# Breathless

## Jesse Book 1

### Eve Carter

*To my lovely family. You are everything to me.*

~*~

# CONTENTS
~*~

*"Life is not measured by the breaths we take, but by the moments that take our breath away."*

-Anonymous

# CHAPTER 1 - WET BJ

### Jesse

"What the fuck are you doing, pervert? Get your hands off my girl."

The hot breath of a large hairy dude was blasting in my face, smelling like shit on a stick. I pulled myself out of the girl's embrace and rolled to my right. I leaned on the cheap plywood bar to steady my woozy legs, while my heart was shooting blood to the body parts needed, in case I had to beat the living shit out of this fucker. Adrenalin was spiking like wildfire throughout my system.

"Mind your own business, asshole. Get the fuck out of my face." I turned my attention back to the girl I was getting close and personal with. Looking like the usual small-town bar girl with her dark-rimmed eyes, long false lashes, and full cherry red lips that moved around the straw in her drink. Lips that made my cock rock hard.

The high had kicked in ten minutes ago with a line of white in the bathroom stall followed by three neat shots of Fireball whiskey. My buddy, Chet, had won a local motocross race and we were here at the Oxford Tap in upstate New York to celebrate. Not like I needed an excuse to shoot coke and down Fireballs, or any booze for that matter. My life sucked. It sucked balls, big time, but right now, all I cared about was how I was going to smash this ugly dude's face three-quarters of the way to the crapper.

The hairy bastard plowed past the ditsy bar girl who got in his way on his trek to find a place for his fist to sink into my face. Chet, my wingman, had disappeared. Out back somewhere with his tongue halfway down the throat of some young chick fresh out of high school with a fake ID. I shouldn't have been so outspoken, but I couldn't help my drunken self. I'm pretty damn charming after downing a few brews, if I don't say so myself.

Fearless, I jutted my chin out towards his face and wrinkled up my nose, "Fuck, that stinks. Dude, your breath smells like a dog just took a dump in your mouth."

"You're a dead man, motherfucker," he raged at me, struggling to get through the packed crowd.

The confrontation between the Beast and me didn't go unnoticed. Two bouncers were already shoving their way past the standard Saturday night regulars, their radar set on us.

The room was spinning. Bodies jammed into the small, dreary, beer-stained area of the local watering

2

hole in this small shit-hole of a town. I didn't care if the Beast hit me or not. I welcomed the thought of the pain of his blows. At least it would blur out the pain in my soul. I teetered. My alcohol-induced, unstable balance may have been an advantage. I staggered out of the Beast's line of fire, just long enough for a strong hand to grab a fistful of my jacket collar from the rear. A heavy hand pulled me down and to the side, pummeling me through the bodies in the crowd. Their drinks crashed to the floor and liquid libations flew through the air, as someone dragged me by the scruff of my neck out the back door of the bar. The same large hand shoved me past the girl I had been chatting up, and I slurred, "Meet me at my truck in the parking lot."

"Shut the fuck up, Jesse!" A gruff voice barked out. I knew all the bouncers at the Oxford Tap.

"Manny? Is that you, bro?" In my drunken stupor I couldn't quite tell who had a vise-grip on my arm, but now I was pretty sure it was my old friend Manny. Manny, the bouncer, to the rescue again. Or so I thought.

*Crap. He was throwing me out.*

"Dude, you got the wrong guy." I gave a wink and a "call me" gesture to the girl gaping at the scene unfurling in front of her dainty face. Nice perky tits bouncing under her top as she walked. Or talked.

"Just saving you from getting your ass kicked again, Jess," Manny puffed, maneuvering his 350-pound frame towards the back of the bar, flinging me around like a rag doll.

"Fuck that. I can take care of myself, Manny. No need to get all violent on me." But I couldn't take care of myself. No way in hell. My motto was to "get fucked up and score as much pussy as possible. Life is short."

Tomorrow, I won't even remember the girl's name—hell, in ten minutes I won't remember her name. What the fuck was her name?

Manny shoved me out the back door and threw me into the alley, letting go of me just in time to send me grinding into the hard, cold pavement. Landing hard, sliding, the rough texture of the cement shaved the top layer of my skin from my face, right about the cheekbone area. Small pebbles of grit wedged themselves into the flesh of my face, small enough that I'm sure I would inflict further pain on myself later, just trying to dig them out with tweezers. My skin peeled, my flesh oozed bright red blood.

*Damn.*

*That's gonna leave a scar.*

Pain signals, fresh and crisp, spiked, like razor sharp lightning into my brain. Hurting like a motherfucker, even in my drug- and alcohol-induced haze. But I didn't give a fuck. I welcomed the pain—no, I savored the pain. As I lay on the ground, my swollen and skinned face absorbed the hardness of the concrete and my eyes rolled back into my head. I just wanted to feel the moment. In my suck-ass life, at least for one instant, the pain reminded me of something—I was still alive.

I groaned.

"God damn fucker, Manny."

I reminded myself to kick his ass the next time I saw him. We were friends back in high school and used to sneak under the stadium bleachers at night to drink beer. Now I drink the hard stuff and he's a washed-up small-town ex-football star, throwing drunks like me out of this crappy bar.

*Fuck.*

My face.

I groaned again and pulled my hands up to my chest. Planting both palms down on the concrete, I attempted to push myself up onto my hands and knees. My stomach wrenched. I hung my head and closed my eyes. It was splitting apart from the inside out, a jackhammer pounding a hundred miles an hour. I shook my head in an attempt to stop the bile from rising in my esophagus, but the shaking motion just provoked the jackhammering.

*Fuuuuuck!!*

*Where's my damn truck?*

I stalled on my hands and knees, hoping to find a small remnant of stability. Crawling over to the brick wall of the building, I used its firmness to help me climb to my feet. Where the fuck had I parked my damn truck? I leaned my back against the cold brick wall, patting my jean pockets with bloody-knuckled hands for the familiar lump of my truck keys.

*Fucking A.* I sniffed, rubbing the back of my hand

against my good cheek and pushed off the wall. I steadied myself with one hand against its surface and fished the keys out of my jeans, squinting, as my left eye was swelling shut.

*I can do this. I can make it to the truck. Just put one foot in front of the other. One foot in front of the other...*

I staggered off in the direction of my truck, or what I thought was the direction. Every step sent new shards of pain throughout my body. Didn't give a fuck. I had it coming to me. I was just a big screw-up anyway.

Shaking fingers pressed frantically at the buttons on the black key fob. A shrill metallic sound-blast ripped the airwaves, making my ears bleed. *Fuck!* I'd hit the alarm button by accident. The truck horn blared loud enough to wake the dead, splitting my head into a million pieces.

Pounding the key fob buttons again, I smashed at the damn device with my thumb, trying to make this acoustic nightmare stop. Whichever bastard invented this annoying feature deserved a swift kick in the balls. Twice.

I jabbed it enough times that the truck horn stopped. But my head didn't stop, it kept on going and going, pounding and pounding. Slumped up against the driver's side, I hunched my torso over the shiny black surface as much as I could. I paused there for a few minutes waiting for the world to right itself on its axis and my breathing to regulate.

My truck—she's a beauty. Raised, big monster

wheels. An F-150, 4x4; full bed, of course. Any man who doesn't have a four-wheel drive pickup truck is a pussy. I stroked the door handle and the smooth surface of the side door panel.

*My old friend Jack was in the console, or somewhere inside.*

I fumbled with the door, cringing in pain with each strain of my sore muscles and swollen hand. Finally, it opened and I fell into the driver's seat sprawled out on my back with my legs still dangling out the door. Reaching my good arm out, I groped around the front seat for the bottle of Jack Daniels I had left there earlier.

*Where the hell you at, Jack?* Stretching and pulling myself further into the cab of the truck on my stomach, I searched around the floorboard area. Bingo. *Hello, Jack ole buddy. Come to daddy.* Downing a large gulp of my fiery friend, I hissed with clenched teeth at the familiar sting in my throat.

*Damn, that feels good.*

I slouched into the cushions of the truck seat, bottle in hand, poised to drink myself into oblivion. I snorted and licked my lips. The salty mixture of sweat and booze assaulted my taste buds. I didn't care. I'd drink my Jack one way or the other. My head fell back against the headrest of the seat. It felt like the seat swayed and shifted beneath me. Slow or fast, it didn't matter. I was down for the ride, wherever it took me.

Shame about losing the girl. I liked her scent. Cute

too. Seemed like a chick that was up for having some fun. The type of girl that spent most nights trolling from one bar to the next, making herself too available for the wrong guys. Those "no-good" guys. Guys like me. I didn't know if she was that hairy bastard's girl or not, but I didn't give a shit. I just wanted to see my dick in her mouth and her head bobbing up and down between my legs.

As I lay there with my eyes closed, fantasizing about bobbing heads, I heard the crunch of light footsteps on gravel, approaching my truck. The sound stopped just outside the door that stood open. Who the hell was bothering me now? If I don't move, they might think I'm passed out. Or dead. Dead would be better. If only I were dead. The silence of the darkness swallowed me for a minute, the truck seat bucked, or so it seemed, and then the silence broke.

"Hey there." The trill of a female voice invaded my foggy senses. I rolled my head to one side and lifted it off the headrest just enough to get a look at girl behind the voice, squinting with one eye open. "Um, you okay?" the voice continued.

My gaze met a pair of black-rimmed, wide eyes blankly staring up at me. Ah, it's the jiggling tit girl from inside the bar, still sucking on that straw. Damn, those lips were hot. "Hey yourself." I tried to sit up, wincing in pain. "What are you doing out here?"

"Um, you told me. You know...at your truck." She twisted from side to side, still holding onto her drink glass. She pinched the straw between her thumb and forefinger, letting it rest for a moment on her lower lip as she spoke. She rolled her eyes in the direction of the bar and then my truck, outlining the path from there to here with her eyes.

Sharp memories of why I landed on my ass on the pavement sliced into my brain. "Shit, your boyfriend is not gonna come out here and go all Frankenstein on me, is he?"

She shrugged her shoulders, still twirling the straw between her fingers, never letting it lose contact with her lower lip. Or tongue. "He's an asshole." She sucked in her cheeks. "You're hot. I like your hair. I like how it falls in your eyes. Is that a tat?" She pointed with her chin at my bicep, the drink straw still attached to her mouth.

"Uh, yeah?" What else would it be? "Why don't you hop up in here? Join me for a drink." I held the bottle of Jack up in the air, gripping the glass neck of it with my good hand.

She shrugged again, cocking her head to the side, and let loose of her straw long enough to run her hand through her long, over-processed bleached blonde hair. She threw one last glance back over her shoulder towards the bar and disappeared around the front of the truck, popping up outside the passenger-side door. I leaned over with a groan, shifting my bottle of Jack to the other hand, and jabbed the door handle open. As she climbed up into the cab, her perky tits bounced as she adjusted herself on the seat. She was petite. Big eyes, big tits, and wet lips begging for me to be impulsive.

I extended the bottle in her direction, and our eyes locked in a rock-solid stare. She tipped her head back and took a long slow swig without taking her eyes off me. I pushed up the center console armrest to make the front seat a bench, and slid over next to her. I watched her lick her plump lips with the tongue I had designs on. That tongue was mine. It would taste like Jack Daniels. I wanted it in my mouth. I moved closer. My face was inches from her lips. I smelled the heavy scent of her cheap perfume. She lowered the bottle from her lips, leaving her mouth open, inviting, still gazing into my eyes. Her wide brown eyes didn't seem to notice the bloodstained gash on my face. Her tongue flicked out of her mouth, wetting her lower lip. My cock twitched in response.

She stared at me with those eyes and said, "Hey, wanna fuck?"

*Oh yeah, game on.*

Sliding my hand around the back of her neck, I filled my fist with her long loose hair and pulled those wet lips onto my mouth, firm and hard. Full lips filled me with the flavor of Jack and her fruity cranberry drink, which I sucked off her teasing tongue. I shoved my other hand up under her loose top searching for the warmth of those perky tits I had envisioned earlier. She pawed and scratched at my chest, pulling and tugging at my T-shirt. She shoved her hand in my crotch as she swirled her tongue deep in my mouth. My cock raged hard and ready, her hand squeezed at it through my thick jeans. *Oh yeah, baby.* I needed more of that, but without the jeans. I sucked her plump lower lip and drew it between my teeth, as I pulled back to readjust my position to get down and dirty with this chick.

She crawled up on my lap, spreading her legs to straddle me. I slid under her and shoved her top up with one hand, pushing her tit up with the other. Her long hair fell around me as she leaned in to smash her mouth onto mine, panting, rocking and grinding on my lap. I tore at her bra, pushing and pulling the fabric, reaching with my mouth to find a dark-circled nipple. *Damn, she's hot.* Her wrenching and grinding moves were making me harder. The firm nub of her nipple rewarded my tongue and I sucked and flicked across it. Her hands couldn't find my hard cock fast enough, as she tore open my belt buckle. I was unzipped in a flash. Heavy breathing filled the cab of the truck with hot vapors. She ripped open my jeans and grabbed my cock, wrapping her warm, small hand around it. Grabbing her face with both of my hands, I shoved her head down to it. She went willingly. I threw my head back, and sucked in a quick breath as those hot wet lips closed around my cock. *That's a girl.*

"Suck it, baby," I whispered. I held her; my hands tangled in all that blonde hair, and watched her head bob up and down on my dick.

I heard a noise.

*Jesus fucking Christ. Who the fuck would ruin a good blow job?*

Someone was crashing my party here in the cab of my truck with Little Lu Lu.

*Shit!* I opened my eyes to the awareness of a large, angry-looking dude swarming up to my truck. Beast Master of the Universe had realized Cha Cha was missing and came out to find her. I was remiss in my duties as a gentleman and had forgotten to get her name. Ah, but now we were about to be introduced.

"Carrie. What the fuck do you think you're doing?"

She screamed.

"Get the fuck out of that truck," he yelled. His face screwed up in anger. "And you, dickhead. *You* are a dead man!"

*Damn, this dude was pissed.* Maybe Lucy, or Carrie, *was* his girl after all? I had her pegged for the town tramp.

"Fuck off, Brian. You don't own me."

"Get your ass out of that truck. I'm tired of you yanking me around every time we have a fight."

Oh fuck, a lover's quarrel and I'm the lucky asshole caught in the middle. His ugly face was screaming at my passenger-door window. The door yanked open and in one swift pull, Beast Master snatched the girl. She squealed and wrenched, as he tore her slight body from the truck by one of her arms.

"You asshole. Get your hands off me," she screamed.

"I can't believe you were sucking this guy's dick. You're nothing but a fucking whore."

The Beast was fuming, and before I could intervene, he hammered her so hard she went flying into the ditch.

"Hey, what the fuck, dude. You don't hit a lady like that," I yelled as I stumbled out of the truck. Before I had a chance to throw a punch at the fucker, two guys grabbed both my arms.

Fuck! The Beast had brought backup. This was not going to turn out well.

"Hallelujah. So you're going to defend the *lady's* honor. How heroic. Only problem here is, she is no fucking lady. She is nothing but a stupid whore."

Oh shit. Hairy Beast was a psycho lunatic. The arrow on the pain-o-meter in my brain arched to the "high level" mark when his two buddies pulled hard on my already sore arm, attached to my already sore shoulder. I think I may have squealed like a girl. Both brutes had a solid grip and stood me up in preparation to be a human punching bag for Beast Master number one. I figured my life was pretty much over now. No need to worry about racing motocross again. Now I could be a whiny bitch about not being able to *breathe* ever again. *Shit! What've I gotten myself into?*

# CHAPTER 2 - Lenny

*Niki*

"American Woman" blasted out in a high, wailing chest voice. No one other than Lenny Kravitz could sing with such an "in your face" style. He was oozing tone. I turned to my best friend Kat and gave her an approving nod. The entire crowd was on their feet, screaming and singing along to the lyrics of the legendary tune we all knew. A monumental smile spread across my face as we all bobbed up and down, hands up in the air, to the music at the MGM Grand Garden Arena in Las Vegas. I was psyched to be here with Kat. It was Spring break, and after studying hard in the last semester of college at UCLA I needed to blow off some steam before finals rolled around.

"This is so cool!" I shouted, trying to be heard above the music.

"I know!" Kat shouted back.

"Lenny is so passionate when he sings." Lenny had the crowd dancing and singing along for the entire set.

"...hot. He's so hot!" Kat shouted again.

"Yes, Lenny is hotter than hot. He is—"

Kat poked a sharp elbow in my side and leaned close so I could hear.

"Not Lenny. The guy over there...check him out. Cute and hot."

"Where, where?" I craned my neck and stood on tippy-toes. I don't know why I paid for the seat. I hardly used it the entire concert.

"One row up and to the right."

"Your big head is in my way. Get out of the way." I laughed as I pushed down on her shoulders. I bobbed and ducked, searching for an opening in the crowd and a clear view of this supposedly hot guy.

"Don't be so obvious. Act like you're not looking." She turned her back towards him while I peeked over her shoulder. The light show pulsed deep indigo blue, to the beat of Lenny's next song, hampering my vision.

"See any cute friends with him? We need one for you and one for me," Kat said. "Here, I know, take a sneaky pic of him." She gave me her iPhone.

"Kat, no. I can't. He's gonna see us." I was too embarrassed to try such a move, but this was right up Kat's alley. "He'll think we're stalkers."

"No, he won't. Who cares, anyway? He's cute!" Kat yelled. The sound of her voice battled the loud music. She grabbed the phone out of my hand and held it high in the air to shoot over the heads of the people in front of us.

"Oh shit." I reached up and pulled her arm down, as

I saw "cute guy" turning in our direction. "He's looking, he's looking." Kat and I grappled with her phone to keep it from falling to the floor. We both dropped into our seats laughing, as Lenny launched into a new song. The epitome of cool, he rocked the place for two hours. The climax of the concert came during an encore jam session when Lenny came down into the crowd, walking the entire perimeter of the arena, singing on a wireless microphone and high-fiving screaming fans in the audience.

The concert ended, leaving us energized and wanting more.

"I wanna dance. Let's hit the clubs." Kat said, still pulsing to the imaginary beat in her head.

"Sure, we're in Vegas, baby. Let's party." We pushed our way out the exit doors and followed the flow of the crowd into a wide hallway that led to the casino area. I was on the last leg of my life as a college student, and although my dad had plans for my future, right now I just wanted to be spontaneous and live for the moment. The words of another one of Lenny's hits churned in my mind. I wanted to "Fly Away."

"Kat, it's always such a blast hanging with you. Hey, you know what we should do?" I turned to her, walking sideways for a moment, as best I could in my strappy black high heels. "We should get an apartment together...this summer. You know, on our own, be free. I'm so fucking tired of living at my dad's house."

"Niki, I'm shocked. You're usually all, 'I gotta be

Miss Logical thinker.' That's the best crazy idea you've had in a long time," she said, clicking along in her heels and swinging her small silver-sequined purse by its chain strap.

"I know...right? Let's frigging do it. I can't wait. We should start looking for a place when we get back home."

Kat stopped abruptly and with a serious face, grabbed hold of my arms. "Just promise me one thing...No PINK walls." She burst out in laughter.

I shook my head laughing. "Okay, I promise. No pink walls, Miss Fancy Pants."

The thought of moving out of Dad's house felt refreshing. No more hyper-focusing on the negative side of things. In the past, I let my anxiety sour my happiness, but things were looking up. Tonight, I shoved all worrisome thoughts aside, stronger and determined to make this time of my life a new beginning.

We cut through the casino floor, weaving our way between the slot machines with all their colorful lights and binging noise. In between the blackjack tables, on a raised stage, a girl in black mesh tights danced seductively to the pulsing beat of a DJ. There's always a party in Vegas.

Two young men in dark suits were handing out free passes to one of the clubs in the casino. Kat took the passes and handed me one. "Woo hoo. This looks like the place for us. The coupon says free Jell-o shots."

"Jell-o shots, what are you...in high school?"

"I just want to have fun, Niki girl. Its Spring break and I don't need an excuse to let loose."

I rolled my eyes and followed her through the door, as we showed our IDs to a very stern-looking door attendant. Standing next to him was a handsome young guy attaching red-colored wristbands to everyone's wrist as they entered.

"Left wrist, please," he said, and showed a beautiful charming smile.

I positioned myself in front of him, my mouth hanging open, gaping at the dimples in his cheeks. I wondered if one of the Chippendale dancers had escaped from the show, as I stood mesmerized.

"Um, thank you, you can go in now," he said, to get me to move it along. Kat shot me a glance and smiled coyly, giving me a little shove. *Oh no, she's up to something.* I could practically see the gears turning in her head.

Kat was very alluring with her petite body and long blonde hair. She had the typical California girl look, was very social and a notorious flirt. I moved aside and she stepped up in front of Mr. Handsome, staring him in the eyes.

"Can I have your wrist?"

Without breaking her stare she said, "Which one? This one, or this one?"

She held each petite wrist up in front of him, still staring.

"Left, please," he said with a smile.

Kat held her left wrist up in front of her chest, while Mr. Handsome proceeded to do his job. As he fumbled to attach the paper wristband, she said, "Here, let me help you. Sometimes it helps to hold it up against something."

She pulled her wrist into her breast, the guy still working on attaching it, until his hands were up against the bare skin of her cleavage. Slowly, she moved her wrist up and down, taking his hands along for the ride. Without batting an eye, she said, "Thank you," in a breathy voice. Flustered, Mr. Handsome exhaled a sigh of relief when I pulled at Kat's arm to make her stop.

"Oh my God, Kat. Leave the poor guy alone."

"What?" she squeaked in a high-pitched voice, following me into the interior of the club. "I was just messing with him. Besides, he's my future husband. He just doesn't know it yet."

"I thought Adam Levine was your future husband."

"Him too. The two of them will have to fight it out over me, but you need to loosen up, have some fun once in a while. I think college fried your brain, girl."

## CHAPTER 3 – Ball Buster

*Jesse*

"You're gonna fucking die, dude," the Hairy Beast barked, as his horrid-looking face moved away from where he had knocked down the girl.

"Hey, man, wait. You don't want to do this. I had no fucking idea she was your girlfriend. We were just partying. Saturday night and all. We've all done that once or twice, right?"

The two gorillas at my sides didn't find much interest in my remark, and tightened their grip on my arms.

In one swift move, the Beast stepped towards me and punched me hard in my abdomen. Luckily, I had anticipated his move and tightened my six-pack just hard enough to withstand the majority of the blow. I leaned forward, faking severe pain. Hairy Beast gloated in my face. I hammered him with a direct kick to his groin. The silence of the night air shattered with screams of pain, as he tumbled to the ground.

I stomped my right heel hard on the top of a boot worn by one of the gorillas, in anticipation of him releasing my arm…but nothing happened. He didn't let go. What the fuck…

*He must be wearing work boots with steel-toed protection.*

The two henchmen slammed me into my truck and one kneed me hard in my stomach, this time knocking the wind out of me.

Bent over and gasping for air, I noticed Hairy Beast coming back to life. He lurched to his feet and my eye caught the glint of polished steel in his hand. The blade of a knife reflected red, then white, then red, then white in the lights of a car…the lights of a car?

I figured I was about to become the Pillsbury Doughboy, poked with a carving knife, when the headlights of a car shone onto the scene of all five of us. The red flashing light on top of a patrol car never looked so sweet. The Beast Master and his flunkies paused like animals frozen in fear for one split second. Car tires ground to a stop, crunching the loose gravel, and the car door flew open.

"Drop the knife and get down on the ground. Now…" someone yelled from the patrol car.

The goons let loose of my arms and scattered in every direction, into the cover of the trees and bushes behind the bar. The officer slammed his cruiser into park and jumped out intent on pursuit, but halted when he noticed the girl cringing and crying, hovering near the truck. He had to let the fuckers run.

Oh my god, I was still alive. I breathed a heavy sigh of relief and stepped over to see if Carrie was alright. The officer stood next to me. "Is she okay?" he asked.

"Not sure. She was hit pretty hard."

"Don't worry, miss, they're gone. Are you hurt? Do you need assistance? Do you need medical help?" The officer spoke slowly to make sure she understood his words.

"I'm okay," she said in a small voice, as she got up on her feet. Carrie sniffed and wiped her eyes with the back of her hand. She had a large red bruise under her left eye. That would be one hell of a shiner tomorrow.

"I saw this girl in trouble, so I tried to help, but the fuckers grabbed me. Thank god you arrived when you did." The officer threw me a cold hard glance that said he would deal with me later. I swallowed hard. I knew what that stare meant.

"He didn't do anything to me." She pointed in my direction. "We were just having some fun, you know..."

I gave her a wide-eyed hint, hoping she wouldn't tell what we were doing in the truck. The officer glanced at me, like "shut up," though I hadn't said a word, and turned his attention back to the girl.

"Thank you, miss. I need your statement. I assume you want to press charges on the guys who did this. Do you know who they are?"

"No. No, it's okay, I don't want to press charges. I'm fine."

"Are you sure, miss? You seem pretty beat up. You shouldn't let them get away with something like this."

"It's okay, really. It was my own fault. I just fell and hit my head on that rock there. I'm so clumsy." She pointed to a rock far away from where she had landed.

"Well, suit yourself," the officer said with a groan. "I'll need to see some identification on both of you; just routine."

The officer ran his usual procedure, checked our IDs, per regulations. Carrie calmed down to his satisfaction and I feared his wrath would be turned on me next.

"Do you need a ride home, miss? I can take you to your residence." He was interrupted by a scratchy voice from the police receiver attached to his shoulder. He reported his location in code to Dispatch and then turned his attention back to Carrie.

She toddled towards the patrol car. "Yes, please, officer, I could use a ride home."

"Alright, take a seat in the back of the car," he said and guided her by the elbow while opening the rear passenger door. "You can wait in the car while I talk with your friend." He shut the door and turned his attention on me. With the red lights still flashing and the headlights of his cruiser shining on me, I leaned against my pickup truck. In a few purposeful strides, he closed the distance between us.

"What the fuck is wrong with you, Jesse? Are you trying to get killed? Who is the girl?"

His eyes glared cold with anger. His voice strained as he yelled through clenched teeth, struggling to keep his voice low so the girl wouldn't hear.

"Hey, Jimmy," I said trying to play it off. "How about a hug for your ol' brother?" I swayed forward like I was gonna give him a bear hug. He shoved me off angrily.

"Get the fuck off me. I'm so sick of you always pulling this crap. You need to get your shit together, man."

"But hey, I was just here minding my own business and—"

"You're fucking drunk, Jesse. You fucked up again and I'm sick and tired of saving your sorry ass. You need to get your shit in one bag, dude. Seriously, I can't always be there for you. You're lucky that Manny called me earlier and told me you were in trouble. Otherwise, I would have picked you up in pieces from that ditch over there tomorrow. You're a fucking embarrassment to me and my job."

Jimmy paced in front of me in his sharp uniform, wearing his gun, with the radio squawking at his shoulder. I leaned back against the cold hard metal of the truck. "Deputy sheriff bails out his drunken-ass brother. There's one for the local newspaper," he ranted. The humiliation on his face would have been devastating to me if I hadn't been too high and too drunk to realize it. But I didn't give a rat's ass right now. All I wanted was another Jack Daniels to burn in my throat, to burn away any semblance of a feeling I might have left in my cold, dead heart.

He reached into the cab of my pickup and snatched the keys from the cup holder, then slammed the door shut. "Get in the patrol car." He fumed. "You are too drunk to drive. I'm taking you home after I bring the girl back to her place. Don't think this is over, either. We'll talk later."

# CHAPTER 4 – Viva Las Vegas

## *Niki*

Inside the O'Hara Club in Vegas, the music was loud, pumping and thumping. The DJ was making his own mixes of the latest house and trance music. We were dressed in typical club-style dresses, short and sassy, and tall shoes, a vice of mine. I was addicted to shoes, and I secretly believed the real reason Kat was my friend was because we wore the same size shoe. And one of the things I loved about Vegas was the parade of hot shoes. Every time I turned around there was another bachelorette party of girls with their magnificently hot "fuck me" shoes. Black, red, zebra stripe, glitter, you name it; and nothing was too over-the-top for Vegas heels.

Kat made a beeline to the bar and picked up her free Jell-o shots. Balancing a beer and four little plastic cups, each filled with cherry-flavored gelatinous blobs, she pushed her way through the crowd to where I had perched my rear end on a red velvet-covered bench seat. Not surprisingly, Kat had flirted her way into a couple of extra shots. She made that move girls with long hair always make when their hands are full, flinging her head so her long blonde hair flipped to her back. She set the shots down on the chrome and glass coffee table. Low tables were situated in between the seating that jutted out into the room, which was bathed in dark, red lighting. The bar itself was opposite the velvet bench seats, and the dance floor was partitioned off from the bar area with reserved tables, available for bottle service customers only.

"Here's your shots. Bottoms up." Kat handed me two and picked up one for herself. She squeezed the bottom and sucked hard to get the gelatinous formation to release from the cup.

"Thanks, hon. I can see you sure know how to suck them down." I laughed.

Everyone had their own technique for removing the wiggly concoction from the tiny container. The only way I knew was to run my finger around the edge first, to loosen it before sucking. Kat downed her shots while standing, too flighty to sit in a place like this. She was stoked from the concert and ready to dance.

"I'm gonna shake some ass out there," she yelled, laughing, as a sharply dressed young guy wearing a black fedora towed her by the wrist to the dance floor. I waved her away.

"No problem. Knock yourself out, girl."

As I licked the sticky off my index finger, I noticed someone's eyes watching me. I removed my finger from my mouth. *Oh shit.* I dropped my gaze to my lap, feeling self-conscious. I pursed my lips and tried to act casual while I wiped the moisture from my finger on the corner of the white cocktail napkin under my drink. From the expression on his face, it was now clear to me why bars gave free Jell-o shots. Guys enjoyed watching all the sucking and licking action.

"You do that very well," A smooth deep voice drew my attention to those watchful eyes. It was him. Holy shit, it was the guy from the concert. I didn't know how to answer that. Was he talking about my finger in my mouth or the way I took the shot? Either way, I was blushing.

"Do you mind if I sit down?" He stood with one hand in the pocket of his dark dress pants, holding a drink glass in the other, as he tilted his head. He had on a black dress shirt, tie, and a vest. And he wore it very well.

"Sure, have a seat." I pressed my knees together and moved over to give him room. I became acutely aware of his close proximity. The heat from his body mixed with the musk of his cologne and the scent wafted in my ·direction each time a person brushed through the crowd. It affected me like a secret pass code on my hormones, and I rotated my upper torso towards him in an open stance. Damn, my body went into autopilot, rapid-firing come-on signals. And if body language could talk, mine would have been screaming. *Why is it so hot in here?* I reached for my drink.

"I think I saw you at the Lenny Kravitz concert

earlier. Did you enjoy it?" He looked awkward perched on the edge of the small red velvet seat. He was tall, at least six feet, had dark black hair, cut short on the sides and held in place on top with gel, a very professional business look but with a younger style.

"Yes, I loved it," I said. "It was such a blast. Lenny really knows how to rock the crowd."

"Yeah, he's awesome. My name is Trevor, by the way." He smiled and my heart skipped a beat, my restless soul rearing its head again.

"Niki," I returned. "Did you come to Vegas just for the concert?"

"No, actually my buddies and I are here for a conference, insurance conference, but we knew about it way in advance and checked out the concerts. When I saw the date for Lenny Kravitz…I had to book it."

"Cool. I'm here on Spring break." I bobbed my head up and down. Did he suspect we had pictures of him on Kat's phone? Shit, we're hopeless stalkers.

"You should join us at our table. My friends and I have a reserved bottle service table by the dance floor. Your friend can come too."

I scanned all the girls sitting down the length of the bench and realized this area was filled with single girls. The single guys were standing near the bar and the perimeter of the dance floor, while the few nice tables had couples.

"Sure, why not?"

I peered around the mash of bodies on the edge of

the dance floor, checking for Kat to signal her to the table. The club wasn't very big, so it was easy to find her. I gestured, with a wave of my hand, to join us at the table nearest to the DJ booth.

As Trevor and I approached the table, his friends gallantly made room for us to have a seat in the booth, and Trevor slid in next to me.

"Where're you from?" I asked.

"San Francisco is where my casa's at," he said sipping his gin and tonic, "but I'm almost never there. My job constantly takes me on the road these days. Haven't been home for the last three weeks. How about you?"

"Los Angeles. Finishing up my last year of college. So...insurance business, you said?"

"Yep. My grandpa was in insurance, my dad and several of my cousins are in insurance, so it was in the cards for me to do the same."

"That's really nice. My dad is a lawyer. All he talks about is how he wants me to go to law school and eventually work at his company. Honestly, I loathe the thought of working for my dad. Besides, I'm more of the creative type, you know?"

"Sure, but being a lawyer is not the worst—"

"Hey, who's gonna buy a thirsty girl a drink?" It was Kat, with the perfect interruption. I could use a break from the conversation.

"There you are. Come sit next to me," I called out. Kat fell into the circular booth, breathless from dancing, as I introduced her to Trevor and his friends.

We all scooted in to fit and Kat elbowed me under the table. Dipping her head towards mine, she whispered into my ear, "Remember, what happens in Vegas stays in Vegas."

"Right," I thought, glancing in Trevor's direction, but I had no intention of doing anything crazy and wild tonight. As exciting as a Vegas night in bed with a hot guy like Trevor sounded, I was not that kind of girl. Besides, I was sort of spoken for already. It was a little complicated. Jason was his name, the new guy in my dad's law firm.

*"Honey, I have found the perfect guy for you."* That was the announcement my dad had surprised me with a while ago over breakfast. *"Just let him take you out on one date. I promise you that you will like him. He is a very nice guy."*

My dad was right. Jason was a nice guy, but that was also the problem. He was nice...well, nice and boring. Most girls would have considered themselves lucky to date a guy like him. He was good-looking, smart, educated, with a great job and a bright future but...to me, he was about as exciting as doing the laundry. I wanted more out of life than just being a lawyer's wife. I had big dreams and hopes for my future, and sadly for Jason...and my dad...Jason wasn't included. I had to find a way to tell them both, which would not be an easy task. Lawyers like to get their way. But moving out of my father's house and getting a place with my best friend would be the first step in the right direction.

I glanced over at Kat sitting on a guy's lap, downing tequila shots with her hands behind her back. I shook my head and smiled. She caught my gaze and smiled back with a wink. I knew it would be one hell of a summer.

## CHAPTER 5 – Thunder Ridge

### *Jesse*

"Hey, man. We need to talk." Jimmy handed me a Coors Light. I was watching a motocross race on ESPN on his flatscreen. *Shit*. The tone of his voice didn't sound good. I knew I had fucked up, but come on, give me a break.

"Yup. Whassup?" I said, keeping my stare on the TV.

Jimmy sat on the edge of the chair next to the couch, resting his elbows on his knees. He seemed pissed that I wasn't paying attention to him.

"Shut that fucking thing off." I shot the remote at the TV and the screen went black. "Listen to me, man." The timber in his voice rose a level. I tossed the remote aside and flung my head back against the couch.

"So…"

"You fucked up again the other night with that chick outside the bar and all…look, I was thinking. Since you're not going back to racing any time soon, I was sort of discussing with Sarah that maybe it would be good for you with a change of scenery."

I stared at the ceiling, searching for something to say. I was dead inside. My life was tearing apart all around me. I had nothing to say. I knew he was right, but I didn't want to deal with this shit right now.

"I think you should go on a trip for a few months. Get your shit together, get a new perspective on things, you know. I was thinking, maybe you could go to California and help Uncle Kenny. I talked to him…"

"What? You called Uncle Kenny? I'm not a fucking charity case."

"It would only be for a while, maybe the summer. He could use some help. You owe him, Jesse, and besides, I can't have you around the house here all summer. Sarah's mood swings are crazy because of her pregnancy and I'm caught in the middle between you two. I've got a baby coming. I can't…"

"Go ahead and say it, Jimmy, you can't have a drunk around the baby."

I closed my eyes and pursed my lips. My own brother was kicking me out.

"That's not what I meant," he growled. A moment of silence hung in the air and then his expression softened. "Kenny said he could use some help getting his new bar off the ground. Just call him, will you?" he pleaded.

"Fuck you."

Jimmy furrowed his brow in anger. I was in the habit of pissing off people these days and he was no different.

"Aaargh! You're such an asshole, Jesse." He jumped to his feet and paced the room as he raged on. "With the baby coming, I need to make sergeant this year and I can't do that with you fucking things up. If you stay here in Thunder Ridge, it's just a matter of time before another night like the other... One more fight, Jesse and I'll be arresting *you*. One more girl and before you know it, someone's pressing charges, serious charges, like assault. You had better get your shit together, man, that's all I have to say."

"Oh, I know." I let out a breath. "It's always the same thing with you, isn't it? Perfect Jimmy the cop. Always doing the right thing. The big hero of the family. The good guy, right? Well, I'm not as perfect as you are. I know I'm the black sheep and you want me the hell out of your life. You're so fucking afraid I'm going to destroy your career that you can't even stand by your own blood."

"That's not true and you know it." He pushed his hand through his hair. "I just want you to grow the fuck up and stop being such a dickhead all the time. Go help Uncle Kenny, get some Cali sun and come home when training for next season starts." He rubbed the back of his neck with his hand, and then let it fall limply to his side. Arguing with him was hopeless. He had already made his decision. His back was to me as he was about to walk out of the room.

"You've got two weeks to pack your shit and get

out." He exhaled and walked out. I hung my head down to my chest. The beer can sat untouched on the coffee table in front of the couch.

Deep down, I knew Jimmy was right. I was a fuckup and I owed Uncle Kenny. I couldn't blame Jimmy for his bossy behavior towards me. It wasn't his fault, really. He had to take over as a father role model back when Dad died. He was only a damn kid himself, robbed and deprived of his childhood, forced to fill the shoes of a grown man much too early in life. And Uncle Kenny, he stepped up when Dad died, and helped too. Hell, what else could he do, it was his only brother who had died and he felt responsible to care for us and Mom. He brought us bags of groceries when Mom couldn't manage. He paid our electric bill to get the lights turned back on when Mom didn't have enough money. He showed us how to ride motorcycles and how to handle a wrench to fix our bikes.

Uncle Kenny helped out for about a year after Dad's death, as far as I could remember. Hell, I was only eight at the time. Jimmy remembers more than I do. Uncle Kenny taught us to race motocross. If it wasn't for him I would never had gotten into racing. We even built a dirt track on our acreage with tight turns and berms. Life was great up until…that day he was no longer there. Didn't even say good-bye, just left us, and that's when Mom got depressed, kept to herself most of the time after that. But still, if it wasn't for Uncle Kenny helping after Dad died, we would have ended up in foster care, or worse.

*~*~*

It was the end of May and I had better get the hell out of Jimmy's house before he blew a gasket. I had decided to take Uncle Kenny up on his offer to stay with him out in California, but only for the summer. Despite all the great things I'd heard about California, the sun, the sand, the beach, I didn't look forward to LA girls, or LA guys for that matter. From what I gathered, the entertainment capital of the world created superficial people. Shallow chicks obsessed with their fifteen minutes of fame and a desire to spend someone else's money. And egocentric, hollow guys who never saw the world beyond the tip of their nose. To me they were all just bitches with too much drama for my liking.

My trusted pickup truck was loaded with all my shit—well, the important stuff I needed for one summer. By my estimation, I was in for a five-day drive. I didn't mind, driving calmed my nerves, and besides, I needed my own wheels once I got there. I didn't want to put out Uncle Kenny any more than necessary. I'm not that much of a jerk. He was doing me a solid, giving me a place to stay and a job.

I sat in the driveway, ready to take off, Jimmy and his wife waving. It was the big fake farewell scene and everyone made me promise to call, or at least text. I looked down at my left hand loosely gripping the steering wheel. I squeezed as tight as I could, but the stiffness remained from the accident. Damn, not a good grip.

"The recovery could take up to nine months," the doc had said.

What the fuck was I going to do with myself for nine months if I couldn't race or even train? This was such BS. All my training and sacrifice just flew out the window that day when I crashed. One maneuver on the bike that I had done millions of times suddenly went wrong.

My heart sank. There was nothing left to do but put the truck in reverse and leave. Who knew, maybe Jimmy was right. Maybe a change of scenery would help. I sure as hell doubted it.

# CHAPTER 6 – Tequila Slammer

### *Jesse*

Most of the first day on my road trip to California, I brooded about my life. Driving soothed my soul. Watching bikers passing by brought back memories of riding my bike out in the open, the wind blowing past my body, I was invincible. It made me feel alive. Riding was my passion, my fire, my life. *Damn.* The thought of losing it all clenched at my gut like a vise grip. What if I never gained back the full function of my hand? What if I could never race in competition again? Maybe I should just break out the rocking chair now and reminisce on the career that was. Maybe that was how my book ended, washed up, pissed off, and not handling it well. *Fuck that shit.* I refused to accept it, but that's how I had spent most of my days lately.

I cranked up the radio and blasted my favorite rock station, the harder the better. If I couldn't drown my sorrows with booze while driving, I was hellbent on numbing myself with music. Later, when the familiar radio stations faded and radio static was eroding my eardrums, I hooked up my iPod, leaned back in my seat, and drummed my fingers on the steering wheel to the beat of a familiar song. The tires of my truck ate up the gray ribbon of pavement as the first day faded into the next.

Two days later, this driving crosscountry shit no longer seemed like such a good idea. I was just outside Denver, Colorado, on Interstate 70. My plan was to make it into Denver and find a room for the night. Fuck it. My ass was numb. I couldn't take one more minute in this truck. I pulled off the Interstate in Bennett, Colorado, into a gas station, and used my cell phone to Google a cheap motel for the night. Bennett looked like a nice town, one with good neighbors, people who cared about each other, the kind of hometown that was remembered with nostalgia by those who had left it behind.

I swiped my finger across the screen and "bingo," I'd found a motel. After filling up the tank, I disposed of the many empty potato chip bags and beef jerky wrappers that had littered my truck. It was a short drive to the motel. I nosed into the parking space in front of a dismal building and a glowing red neon sign in the window of the adjacent storefront caught my eye— "The Corner Pocket." *Hell yeah!* This looked like a good place to get a beer, and it was right next door.

I stepped out of my truck, my body stiff from the drive, and I walked like an old man into the office to check in. Old motorcycle injuries have a way of messing with your muscles like that. *Fuck.* I couldn't wait to feel the cool brew sliding down my throat along with a chaser or two, or four, or maybe more of Jack. I got the room key but didn't even bother putting my bag inside, or moving my truck. I headed straight for the bar. I figured they had a burger on the menu to go with my liquid dinner of booze.

It was late when I walked into the dim light of the Corner Pocket. A few locals sat hunched over the bar, nursing their beers. A dreary country song was playing and the piped-in music was only interrupted by the click of pool balls in the back. A guy in cowboy boots and a girl in a white tank top and cut-off jean shorts played a slow game on the tattered green velvet.

I slid up to the bar and raised a finger to signal the bartender. He yelled to a girl at the other end of the bar, "Holly, customer." I rubbed my face with the heels of my hands, tired from driving. A cute young woman with long brown hair and bangs that fell in her eyes ambled over to where I sat.

"What'll it be?" she asked with her pouty lips. She stared blankly, a few strands of her bangs catching in her eyelashes. She sure as hell didn't look thrilled to be working in this dive. She tossed her head to move the hair out of her eyes, while her hands were busy finding a beer glass.

"Just give me whatever's on tap and a Jack Daniels chaser."

She walked down to the tap to fill the glass. Her

plump, jean-covered ass twitched as it trailed away. My eyes followed like a tracking device. I liked her ass. It came with nice round tits that busted out of her shirt and a not too tiny waist under that loose top. That was the kind of ass a guy could grab on to. With a beer in her hand, she came back and slapped it on the sticky bar in front of me, dripping a puddle around it.

*Nice rack.*

She held up the shot glass for my chaser and wiggled it in the air. "Neat?"

I nodded and she poured. I downed the Jack first, and then drained half the beer in one gulp. I tapped the rim of the empty shot glass for another, watching Holly drag her teeth over her lower lip. After she poured my second Jack, she leaned forward on her elbows and looked me up and down. Her eyes stopped at my tat. Only part of it was exposed, creeping out from under the sleeve of my T-shirt.

"What's that say?" She cocked her head sideways to read the tat crawling up my arm.

I cut a glance down to my bicep. I reached my left hand across my chest, pushed up the edge of my sleeve enough to expose the entire caption, and said, "Carpe Diem."

We both said "Seize the day" at the exact same time. She laughed and broke a smile.

"Whatcha doing in town? Staying at the motel?" She batted her long eyelashes as she talked and reached down to run a glass through the washing station just under the bar top.

"It's that obvious?" I crossed my arms and leaned on the bar.

"Yup. I can tell outsiders. You have that 'just passing through' look about you."

I snorted and shook my head. "Yeah, you got me pegged." I shoved my hand through my hair. It never stayed in place. It was always falling down in my eyes. I should cut it, but I don't give a damn. I blew out a long breath.

My golden brown liquid friend Jack was melting away the day's tension. It felt good to relax after all the driving and the stress of being on the road. My beer glass was empty by now. She eyed it like she could read my mind. She didn't need to ask, but I answered, "Just keep 'em coming." She twitched away again to refill my beer and I slouched into the back of the tall bar stool until she returned with my drink.

"Thanks. You got a cheeseburger on that food menu?"

"Sure do. A nice juicy half-pounder."

"That sounds perfect...um, Holly?" She batted her long lashes again, their dark length flicking at a wisp of her bangs. That was hot. I felt a twitch in my groin. A little smile quivered at the corner of her mouth and it twitched again.

"Yep, I'm Holly. What's your name, hon?" She stood poised with one hand on her hip and pushed a coaster at me for my weeping beer glass, then turned to put in my order.

"Jesse, and I'm from…"

"No, wait. Don't tell me. Let me guess. I'm pretty good at guessing where people are from." She scoped me out with a sidelong glance. She rose up on her tippy-toes for a minute to peer over the bar, to get a good look at my clothes and, well, my body. I could see her eyes stall at my chest and upper arms. I glanced down at my torso, then back at her. She settled her weight back onto her heels, coming down off her toes, and her tits jiggled. *Nice.* Shit, she'd already eyed my tat, now she was eye-fucking me up and down. This could be promising. She opened her mouth to talk but I cut in.

"Wait, Holly. Let's make this interesting. Me and you, and my old friend Jack, are gonna play a game. You guess where I'm from and if you're wrong, you take a shot. You get three guesses and every time you're wrong, you gotta take a shot. If you guess right, I have to take all the remaining shots. Deal?" I smiled a cocky smile and crossed my arms across my chest.

She pursed her lips, looked up to the left, and twisted her mouth to the side, pulling in her bottom lip. "Hmm. It's time for my shift to end, but okay, hon. I'm game." She reached under the bar and slammed a clean, empty shot glass on the bar in between both of us.

"Uh-uh, girl. Three. You get three guesses. That'd be three glasses, baby." She rolled her eyes and huffed, before dragging two more shot glasses from the wash area under the bar. She pushed them into a neat row and looked up at me.

"Fill 'em." I ordered and raised my eyebrows. She responded to the teasing twinkle in my eyes with a "come on" look, and she filled all three with Jack Daniels. She leaned her weight into her elbows on the bar, screwing up her face like she was thinking hard.

"You know you're gonna lose. I'm pretty fucking good at this." She smiled.

"Bring it." I sat back and waited for her guess.

"You are from…" She paused, her eyes searched the ceiling. "…Alaska."

"Hell no. Do I look like a fucking Eskimo?" I chuckled.

*I got this.*

She dropped her head forward until her forehead almost touched the bar, laughing, and her long brown hair fell down, pooling on the shiny black surface of the bar. I threw my hands up and laughed with her, then slapped my palm down on the bar in front of the row of shots. "You gotta drink." I kept pounding my hand on the surface as I chanted, "Drink, drink, drink. Go on now. You lost, take your punishment." I egged her on. I wanted to watch her take the shot. I wanted to see her toss her head back with her mouth open and her neck exposed, as her long soft hair fell down her back. I felt a tug in my loins. *Come on, baby, just do it already.*

She flipped her hair out of her face as she straightened up from her fit of laughter and tried to

45

settle herself.

"Okay, okay. I got this. You won the first round. But I'm only doing this because I like your tattoo." She reached for the glass at the end of the three neatly lined up in a row and held it up in a salute. "Carpe Diem."

I grabbed one of the shots and held it up. "Carpe Diem," I said, and locked my eyes on her as she tossed her head back and my fantasy was born. It was as beautiful as I had imagined. I wanted my mouth on her neck. I wanted to run my tongue up the length of her soft skin and fill my mouth with her pouty lips. *Damn*. I hoped she would never guess where I was from.

I threw back my shot, quickly, before she could catch me staring, and adjusted myself in my jeans under the bar. She sputtered and coughed from the burn, fanning her face with her open-fingered hands. It was more of a gesture than the need for air. She took the shot like an expert. My mind wandered. What else could she take like an expert? *Fuck*. I had to adjust myself again.

She sucked in her lower lip. "Whew. That burned. But in a good way."

She threw the used glass into the wash area, then turned back and planted both hands on the bar. "Okay, Jesse. You're one for three. Let's go again. I get another try."

"I thought you were good at this," I snickered. I wasn't sure if she was losing on purpose to keep drinking with me. "Okay, guess again. Wait, do you want a hint?"

"No, no." She bounced up and down, waving me away. I watched as the flesh of her tits moved with her. "I don't need a hint. I can get this. I'm good at this. I've worked here for a long time...since...damn, since eleven o'clock this morning. Fuck, I work too much." She giggled as the alcohol worked its way into her bloodstream.

"Uh, am I keeping you from your work?"

"Hell no. I was off half an hour ago. We're just partying together now, sugar. Just you and me."

"Well, then, let's get to partying. Come on now, make another guess." She pushed off the bar and straightened up as if that would help her think.

"Okay. Here goes. You are from...wait, let me hear your accent again."

I pulled back and furrowed my brow. "What the hell? I don't have an accent, *you* have an accent. Shit. Y'all."

"Come on, come on, say, the word car."

"Ca-a-a."

She giggled.

"Say the word, bar-r-r."

"Ba-a-a." She reeled back on her heels in giggles.

"Car-r-r-r. Bar-r-r-r." she enunciated and drew out the sound of the last letter. "There is an 'r' on the end of those words. You have to be from the East Coast, like New York?"

"Nope," I lied. I wanted her to take another shot and

show me that long tempting neck again. She looked puzzled and stared me dead in the eyes.

"Liar."

I rolled my eyes, like the cat that caught the mouse.

She got more vehement and slapped the bar top. "You shit-head! You're from New York, aren't you?" She squealed. "You are devious."

She came around to my side of the bar in a burst and stood next to me, leaning one elbow on the bar. She reached up, groping my head with her fingertips.

"Wait, I feel it." She poked at my scalp again. "Yeah, that's it, right there. I can feel the horns growing as we speak."

I playfully slapped her hand away. As she reeled back, I slipped my arm around her waist and pulled her into me. She smelled good. Sweet, and surprisingly fresh, for working in such a dive. Her long brown hair whipped around me as she teetered forward from the force of my grip. Hot silence brewed between us for a moment before she turned away from me to face the bar for her punishment drink. I ran my hand slowly up and down her back, feeling the curve of her body as it dipped in the small of her back, right above the rise of her rump. I wanted my hand to continue on down her backside, over those tight-fitting jeans, over her ass. I fantasized for a brief moment of pushing her head down and bending her over the bar, her ass up in the air, and mounting her right in the bar. I shook my head. *Get a grip, dude.* It's too soon for that, but later, yeah. I'll tap that ass and she'll let me put my hands all over her. I watched her eye the last shot glass as hardcore lust burned between us.

"New York, huh? How did you guess?"

"I'm psychic."

I raised a brow.

"No, I saw your driver's license when I checked your ID, duh." She rolled her eyes like I was an idiot. Hell, I was, most of the time. I bit my lower lip, my eyes fixated on her ass. I wanted to slap a firm hand on it so bad. I moved my legs apart as I sat on the bar stool so she could stand between them. Damn, having her close to me felt good. I let my leg rub against her warm thighs. The sexual tension between us practically crackled like static electricity. I leaned into her bare arm and nuzzled my nose on the soft smooth skin of her shoulder. The full tactile contact made my fucking dick twitch and I pushed my thigh against the fullness of her body. I stalled there, eyes closed, and drew in a breath with my lips against the coolness of her skin.

She broke my mood and distracted my focus, dragging me back to other more civil thoughts. "That last shot is looking pretty lonely there. I already guessed where you're from, so I won. You have to take the shot."

"Are you bustin' my chops, lady?" I joked.

Still wedged between my legs, she twisted around to face me and slipped her arms loosely around my neck. She tilted her head back and I lunged at her neck, dragging my teeth gently across her skin, then sucking out a kiss.

"Keep doing that and you're gonna get us both in trouble."

"I like trouble. Trouble is my middle name," I mouthed against her neck as I kept my lips connected to her skin. She rolled her head to the side and dipped her head close to mine. I felt her hot breath in my ear.

She stole a glance around the half-empty bar, and whispered in my ear, "You seem like the type of guy who likes danger."

"Mmm, I am." I continued exploring her long neck. "Racing motocross for a living is kind of dangerous."

"Jesse, do you want a little adventure?" she asked in a low breathy whisper. Her teeth teased at my earlobe.

"Mmmm…yeah, but here? Don't you think it's a little risky?" I murmured, eyeing the bar owner almost falling asleep on the other end of the bar.

"Otherwise it wouldn't be an adventure."

She pulled back and slipped her hand into her front jean pocket, retrieving a little yellow pill with the imprint of a smiley face on it. She wiggled it between her thumb and forefinger, nervously glancing around the bar, then hid it in the palm of her hand.

"Do you like this kind of adventure?"

"Yeah, baby. I'm down."

"Okay, you'll need a tequila slammer to go with it."

"What the fuck is a tequila slammer?" I was annoyed when she pulled away from me. She left me all raw and edgy-feeling, like my shit was all hanging out. I wanted that feeling back. *Damn it.*

I swiveled around on my stool as she stepped down to the end of the bar.

"Motorcycle rider, right?"

"Yup." I nodded. She grabbed a black motorcycle helmet that was sitting at the end of the bar. It was the half helmet type. No facemask.

"Here, put it on," she directed as she disappeared around to the other side of the bar.

"What the hell is this shit?" I asked, holding the helmet like "I'm not putting this crap on my head." She slammed a bottle of tequila and a shot glass on the bar. I stared blankly, wondering if she was going to make me drink out of this nasty old helmet or something. She jumped up on the bar and spun around on her behind until her legs were dangling over the edge of the bar on my side. She spread her legs open and slid over so I was sitting right in front of her, her legs open in a wide V.

"Put it on," she commanded.

I drew back with a crooked smile. "Say what?"

"Just put the helmet on and play along. You'll like it, I promise."

"OK, but I warn you, I'm a virgin so be gentle," I mocked.

She pushed on my shoulder and spun me on my stool so I had my back to her. I put on the helmet.

"OK, now lean back so your head is resting on the

bar right between my legs."

I complied. She scooted back a little as I laid my head back between her wide-open legs.

"OK, sugar. Close your eyes and open your mouth," she said, holding the soda dispenser in one hand.

I could hear the clink of the tequila bottle and the next thing I felt was wetness in my mouth. My eyes popped open and I saw the tiny yellow pill drop into my mouth along with the tequila and some Sprite. She grabbed my head, helmet and all, with both of her hands and slammed my head hard on the bar.

"That's a tequila slammer," she said, as the helmet made a loud bang.

I damn near choked as the Sprite and tequila fizzed wildly inside my mouth. I swallowed in one huge gulp, gagging, gasping, and laughing all at once. She leaned over my head and kissed me upside down, running her tongue around the edge of my lips.

She let loose of me and I sat up. I damn near fell off the stool but it was all in good fun. I stood up, and pushed the stool back. I took off the funky old helmet and shoved it down the surface of the bar, out of our way. She sat in front of me with her legs spread wide open. It wouldn't take long for the XTC to kick in. My dick and I wanted this girl naked. Immediately.

"My turn," she said.

She wet her lips, opened her clenched fist in front of me, revealing another little yellow pill for herself in the palm of her hand. Before she could pop it in her mouth

I grabbed her wrist and held her arm in place. She didn't move. Without breaking our glance, I brought her open palm up to my face. I opened my mouth and touched the tip of my tongue to the pill. It adhered to the moisture on my tongue. With a jerk I pulled on her wrist, so she would fall forward into me. She moved in my direction, and I wrapped my arm around her waist. I held her wrist, pinning her arm behind her back. It forced her to arch up and her lips parted in a reflex action. A little gasp erupted from her throat and I shoved my tongue in her mouth, pushing the little pill off the tip for her. I paused for a second and she swallowed. My goddamn cock was getting thicker inside my jeans. *Damn, this girl was hot.* She came at me hard, shoving her tongue in my mouth, twisting into our kisses, pulling her fist into my hair. I could have taken her right there on the top of that dirty, sticky bar, but I figured we had better get out before being thrown out.

"Let's get the fuck out of here," I said breathless.

"I thought you'd never ask," she said, and bolted off the bar to the back side, where she snagged her purse out from under the bar. We split in a flash and headed for my motel room next door.

# CHAPTER 7 – Fly Away

## *Niki*

The sharp ripping sound from the oversized tape dispenser pierced the air in my bedroom. Packing boxes were stacked in the corners near the pale pink walls. Turquoise blue contrasted with black accents on the fabric of my bedspread and curtains to create a fresh modern design. Clothes from the closet, with hangers still on them, lay over the back of my study desk chair. Shampoos and other toiletries from my bathroom were piled on top of the dresser, waiting for Kat to put them in a box. I looked at the teetering pile of toiletries, looked over at Kat sitting on the bed, then looked back at the pile and exhaled, knowing the box wouldn't get filled anytime soon. I walked over to a box I had begun to fill and bent over to pick up a soft plush item from the floor.

"Why are you taking that old thing?" Kat's head popped up from her iPhone screen. She frowned and looked perturbed at me. I knelt down and placed a large white teddy bear with a red ribbon around its neck into the cardboard moving box on top of pairs of my endless collection of shoes. I closed the lid and sealed it with tape.

"It's a keepsake and besides, I need him to cuddle with in bed at night when I can't get a date."

Kat looked up again, long enough to roll her eyes. "The shoes you need, because we wear the same size, but the bear is kid stuff. You're going to be a lawyer, for Christ's sake. Lawyers don't sleep with teddy bears. Just leave it."

Kat sat with her back propped up against the headboard of my bed and her legs bent at the knees, barking out orders, while posting a status update on Facebook.

"Hey, did he ever call you?" Kat asked, as she finally looked up from her phone.

"Who?"

"Trevor. The hot guy from Vegas."

"Oh...that guy. No, haven't heard from him yet. He said he'd call when he is back in LA later this month."

"Cool. I liked him."

"Yeah, I guess he was kind of cute."

"He was hot and ten times more fun than boring Jason. When are you going to tell him?"

"Tell him what?"

"That you're breaking up with him, dummy. You're still breaking up with him, right?"

"One thing at a time, hon. It was hard enough letting my dad know that I'm moving out of his royal empire."

I had lived at home my entire college career, with

my dad and his ridiculously much-too-young second wife. Her name was Cinnamon. Yeah, that's right, she had a stripper name. Twenty years younger than my dad, with a rockin' hot body and a stripper name.

When they married in Vegas six years ago, there was no way in hell I was going to call her Mom. The name Mom deserved respect and I didn't have any for...Cinnamon. I cringed at the thought of saying her name out loud in parental situations. Like when I had to introduce her to my high school teacher, senior year, at Open House night. "Hello, Mrs. Hubert, this is my...er...step-mom, Cinnamon." How humiliating.

I never blamed Dad for wanting to remarry after Mom's death. He was still a young man and I wanted him to be happy. Do whatever it would take, follow your heart and be happy. That's what Mom would have wanted.

I thought it would be hard leaving the house where Mom lived with us, but ever since Cinnamon arrived, her presence changed the soul of the house. It was like Mom's essence had been overshadowed by Cinnamon's personality. At first, I was angry at Cinnamon for invading my mother's house. Mom's memories were ingrained in the rooms where we all lived and interacted with warmth and love for each other. I was angry at Dad too, but I never dared showing him, so I took it out on Cinnamon. Blaming her was the easy way out.

It was my senior year in high school. I was younger,

more impulsive and full of drama, but I'm older now; and especially since graduating from college, I've felt ready to let go of all the old anger. I was tired of carrying around the pain and the hurt. It was weighing me down and now I was ready for some changes in my life.

"Kat, you know...that plan about me being a lawyer...going to law school and all." I grabbed another folded box and assembled it for more shoes. I sat down cross-legged on the floor at the foot of the bed and wrote the word "bedroom" neatly on the outside of the box with a large black Sharpie marker. Kat barely heard me, consumed with social networking on her phone.

"Hey, hey, check this out." She jumped up to her knees and crawled to the foot of the bed, laying out flat on her stomach, dangling her phone screen over the edge of the bed to show me a post on Facebook. "Lisa just posted that her and Carly are going to a club on Saturday. We should go."

"Kat, did you even hear what I just said?" I waved the pen in the air as I spoke.

"Oh what? Sorry, you were saying..." She pulled her phone back out of my face and sat up on the bed cross-legged.

"Well, I have decided to take a year off before I apply to law school. I've been doing a lot of soul searching this last year. Now that I've finished this milestone in my life, which I did for my dad, you know…" I wrung the black marker in my fidgety hands.

Kat cocked her head to the side, looking at me with the concern of a true friend. "What is it, Niki? You can tell me, girlfriend."

"There is this one thing I always wanted to give a shot. I know it's crazy but…I've been thinking about going to fashion school. You know, learn fashion design."

"What? That's fantastic. You should totally do that…but what does your dad say about this? I mean, you already have a four-year degree from a great college. Those fashion schools aren't really an academic institution, they are…well, they are training schools. Your dad will kill you if you don't go to law school."

"I know, I know." I cringed and furrowed my brow. "But this is what I want to do. At least, I think it's what I want. Anyway, I already told him that I needed a year off school, which he seemed to be okay with. I can't keep living my life for someone else."

"Hey, babe, I'm with you. I know where you're coming from. All I want to do is sing and perform. Talk about disappointed parents. You should have seen their reaction when I told them I wanted to be a singer. They would've been happier if I'd announced I was gay." She sat back on her knees, waving her cell phone in the air as she spoke. "Well, they were bummed at first but they support me now. I *am* damn talented, you know. It won't be long before I get discovered by some hot music producer." She laughed and tossed her long blonde hair over her shoulder, while swiping her finger to open a new app.

If anyone could understand my need for creativity, it was Kat. She had started college with me freshman year, but quit to pursue a career as a makeup artist. After about a year of working in the MAC cosmetics store, giving makeovers, she'd had enough of uptight customers and decided to focus on her true passion, music. Kat was a singer-songwriter by heart, continually writing new sultry songs and playing her guitar. Thanks to her fabulous networking skills, she managed to secure gigs around town in small venues, performing her original songs.

"I wish I had your parents. They're so cool with their 'old hippies' style. I'm tired of fulfilling someone else's dreams." I picked at a loose thread on the carpet where I sat on the floor. "I have to explore this part of my personality…no, my *being*. It's time for me." I stood up and grabbed another roll of clear packing tape from the desk. "So I was thinking, I could take classes at the Fashion Institute in LA."

"You mean FIDM. That would be awesome, and it's not that far from our new place."

"Exactly. What's to lose? And if it doesn't work out, no problem. I'll apply to law school, satisfied that I gave it a shot, and everybody is happy."

"Hell yeah. That sounds like a good plan."

"God, I hope so. Thanks for the support, hon." I

leaned over the bed and gave Kat a big hug.

I was shocked that Dad was okay with me taking a year off before law school. He said he had done the same thing at my age and it was the best thing he had ever done. It gave him the energy he needed to later finish top of his class and become the "go-to" lawyer for actors, singers, and songwriters in Hollywood. He always said I should follow in his footsteps and become a lawyer, even offered for me to work in his firm once I had my law degree. But this was his dream. Not mine. Unfortunately, my dad was not a person you said "no" to very often. He was of Italian descent, a very passionate, powerful, and stubborn man. Growing up I never dared confront him, or go against his wishes. He was all the family I had left, so I hit the books and studied hard.

As the years ticked by in college, I matured, and realized I had been suppressing an artist's soul. I had a passion for color, form, and fashion design. Living with Dad and his rigid, sequential, logical thinking had squelched the creative spirit in me. He couldn't help it, he had to be that way, he was a lawyer; but I had inherited opposite attributes from Mom. She was beautiful, graceful, and had been a talented interior designer. I thought if I were half as beautiful and half as talented as she, I would be happy.

Kat was back to messaging on Facebook. "Come on, Miss Social Networking butterfly. Put that damn phone away and help me carry these boxes down to my car." I plopped a medium-sized box on the bed in front of her. She shoved her phone in the back pocket of her white shorts.

"Let's do this."

# CHAPTER 8 - Ecstasy

## *Jesse*

Wow, my mind melted into a euphoric bliss from the little yellow pill Holly had dropped into my mouth earlier. I pulled her close to me and wrapped my arm around her waist, her thick thighs bumping up against mine, as I guided her towards my motel room located just across from the bar. Her soft dark hair swished against my body in the night air as we walked. I stopped outside the door, transfixed on all that dark long hair. I was mesmerized. I reached out my hand and stroked it, feeling the sensation of its softness on my fingertips. My sense of touch was embellished. I picked up a silky lock and rubbed it between my fingers. It felt like liquid.

*Ah, this was the shitz.*

I reached out with both of my hands, tousling my fingers in her hair, pushing it up and swirling it around on her head like a crazy man, absorbed by my own motions.

She giggled and rolled her eyes.

"Your hair." I kept swirling. "Your hair is sooo nice. I love your hair. I want to rub it all over my body. I want to wrap myself up naked in your hair..."

She knew it was the effects of the drugs making me act stupid. I didn't care. She didn't care. She reached up and pulled my hands out of her hair and we fell into a long heavy kiss, which felt fucking awesome on my lips, but I needed to get inside the damn room before I exploded on the sidewalk outside.

"You got the key, sugar?" She leaned against the red brick wall waiting for me, twirling her finger in her hair.

I fumbled in my pocket and found the plastic key card. As I rubbed my fingers over the smooth plastic card, with its slick glass-like surface, it felt lustrous, more uniform than anything I had ever felt on earth. I rubbed it between my thumb and forefinger, hyper-focused on its texture.

"Give me that," she said, and snatched it out of my hand, unlocking the door. I laughed and she grabbed a fistful of T-shirt at my chest and pulled me through the door. Damn, I was in a happy mood all of a sudden. No, I was in a goddamn fucking fantastic mood. Oh, fuck me. I loved this room. I loved the bed in this room. I loved the stained green carpet in this room. I loved the curtains and those tiny little yellow flowers on the curtains in this goddamn awesome room. This was the goddamn most awesome motel room ever.

We fell into the room laughing and I kicked the door

shut with my foot. We danced around in the short space between the door and the bed, our bodies tangled together, sidestepping our way to the edge of the bed. Clawing and tearing at each other's clothes, we fell onto the cheap floral bedspread. It was a damn small room, but I didn't give a shit. I loved it and I was on the verge of diving into a tight, wet pussy. All I cared about was getting that beautiful round ass up in the air, so I could rock that pussy with my hard cock. *Fuck*. If her hair felt magnificent, imagine how intense her hot little cunt would feel?

*Where the hell's my condom?*

I had a raging hard-on burning a hole in my jeans. Panting and breathless, I jumped up from the bed and tore off my shirt. Holly pulled off her loose top in one sweep over her head, while I kicked off my shoes and stripped out of my jeans, underwear and all, relieved to set myself free.

She wiggled on the bed, disrobing, and caught sight of my massive erection, springing up to the ceiling. "Damn, baby. You're hot as hell. You need to fuck me quick with that thing."

*Hell yeah.*

My blood rushed through my veins, like a bat outta hell. I bent over, digging in my jeans on the floor for my wallet; it contained the condom I needed. I couldn't wait another minute. I stood up, looked at her sitting there on the bed, and pushed my hand up through my hair. Every sensation felt incredibly intense, my skin prickling with the impressions of a million pins.

I growled. *Oh shit, did I really do that out loud?* All she had left on were her black lace panties. I fell in love with the intricate lace design on those panties, as it seemed to expand and rise up off her skin. She sat with one arm across her breasts, covering her nipples. She pulled the length of long dark hair to one side, exposing her neck and letting her head hang down. She pushed and caressed her own breasts with her hands. My cock hungrily jerked and my blood surged, rocketing fire through my veins. I reached out with both hands, to pull the panties down her hips. She lay back slowly and stretched out, throwing her arms up over her head, as I pulled. *Oh my fucking God.* This was going to be crazy hot sex. I exhaled. My entire body vibrated and waves of euphoria washed over me. My heartrate accelerated and I reveled in it.

*This was some fucking good shit.*

She rubbed one hand across her tits, while the other slid down her stomach and rubbed at her trimmed mound. She rolled her head to one side and licked her lips.

I crawled onto the bed on my knees and ran one hand up the inside of her leg, pushing it open as I touched the thick meat of her thigh. Her skin felt incredibly smooth. The firmness felt good in my hand. I squeezed, letting the response fill my brain. She moaned.

*Damn, this chick was ready.*

I pushed my hand up further and slipped my fingers into her folds. The slippery wetness felt incredible. She bucked and thrust her hips in the air as I swirled my fingertips deeper into the folds of her skin. She was so soft and wet I thought my fingers would meld right into her skin. I wanted to swim into her sea and roll on the waves all night.

My mouth fell open and I was impulsively drawn down on her by the scent of her pussy, tingling in my nose.

*Fuck, I gotta taste her.*

I wanted her sweet raindrops on my tongue, shooting into my mouth with her ragged orgasm. I shoved my face in her pussy and grabbed her ass with both hands. She felt like butter on my tongue.

*Oh fuck, she did taste good.*

I flicked and swirled with my tongue. She wrenched and moaned, hitching her breath. The sounds of her pleasure were deep and primitive, each tone a call my body answered with a primal drive. I licked that pussy and finger-fucked her until she screamed out her orgasm, and my cock was a red-hot steel shaft, aching for relief.

*Oh motherfucking God. I wanted to drive my cock deep in her.*

My mind reeled with outrageous carnal lust as I struggled not to let my sexual desire sweep me under just yet. I had to get the goddamn condom on first. I left her panting on the bed and reached for the nightstand. I picked up the condom and ripped open the package. My heart was racing, my mouth felt dry. I fumbled with putting it on. My mind was pierced with one razor-sharp thought, with that one damn sensation I craved. I was gonna fuck her breathless.

She moved towards me on the bed, her movements triggering animalistic reactions. I pulled her by her ankles to the edge of the bed and flipped her over.

"I'm gonna fuck the shit out of you, baby," I panted.

She gasped and squealed. That high-pitched kind of girl moan always spiked my adrenaline in a flash and I knew I had to fuck her bent over the edge of the bed. I grunted and drove my hard cock into that sweet-ass pussy.

*Fuck yeah.*

She was still a fine wet mess. I held her hips and pounded her hard. The pleasure of her tight pussy all around me was off the charts. The rush was so fantastic, so extreme I thought the top of my head was going to blow off. Her body rocked and jolted hard, as I raged inside of her. My awareness of reality was slipping away with each frantic thrust and stroke.

*Oh my fucking God!*

I felt the tidal wave coming; it was a motherfucking monster. This time I didn't hold back, I surrendered and let it take me under, as I exploded my cum inside of her.

"Oh God," I gasped, between breaths. "That was fucking intense."

She rolled over onto her back and threw a bent arm up, resting her forearm on her forehead, pulling large breaths of air into her lungs.

"Wow. Yeah, intense is the word." She was still reeling from the pounding she took.

I fell onto the bed beside her. My heart was still racing and my skin tingled like it was on fire. The effects of the drug were at their height. I felt alive. I was euphoric, and happy with the entire world. Nothing could stop me, I was invincible. I was a goddamn sex god, with enough testosterone to fuck this pussy all night. And I had every fucking intention of doing just that.

*Goddamn, my mouth was dry.*

I jumped up and ran into the bathroom. I turned on the cold faucet and cupped my hands under the waterfall, scooping handfuls into my mouth. I couldn't get enough. The cool water splashed and trickled down my chin as I gulped for dear life. Jesus, even the water hitting my skin felt like a new sensation, like I felt it for the first time. I threw handfuls on my face, not caring that it sprayed onto the floor. I ran my open hands down my face to accentuate the effect.

I carried two cups of water from the bathroom and placed them on the nightstand. Holly grabbed one, eagerly gulping it down, soothing the dry-mouth side effect of the XTC. I stared at her tits as she drank. They looked amazing. Round, plump, and the nipples were large and hard from arousal. She had the kind of nipples that were surrounded by an exceptionally large dark area. The urge to feel those large nipples in my mouth hit me like a ton of bricks, and my cock rose to an intensified erection. Those large pink nipples needed to be in my mouth, like right now.

*Jesus fucking Christ.*

I had to take her again, driven by another one of the drug-induced cravings to slam my cock deep inside of her. I was going to fuck this girl all night long.

Holly reached over the edge of the bed and dug something out of her purse from the floor.

"We need some music," she said. She popped her iPod into the docking station of the clock radio at the side of the bed and put on her favorite playlist of slow jamz. I crawled on top of her and pushed a handful of tit into my mouth.

We lost ourselves in the music for hours and I pounded her again and again, fucking her in every way imaginable, until the plateau of my high tapered off. We went at it all goddamn night, kissing, licking, fucking, talking, and feeling the music with more awareness than we thought possible. But eventually we crashed into exhaustion, and fell asleep.

*~*~*

*Fuck, what's that horrible noise?*

I reached over a long-haired girl next to me in bed and yanked the iPod out of its docking station. Reality

69

sank in as I looked around the cheap motel room. The time on the clock reminded me that I had better get my ass on the road and drive, if I wanted to make any progress towards California today.

I rolled out of bed without a sound and found my clothes strewn all over the damn floor. I pulled on my jeans and shoved my feet into my shoes as best I could in the fatigued aftermath of the night before. I glanced at the girl, entwined in crumpled sheets, her nice ass partially exposed.

*Damn, I fucked the shit out of her last night.*

I scribbled a short note on the motel notepad and left it on the nightstand sitting under her iPod with a twenty dollar bill.

*Holly,*
*Had to hit the road. Long trip ahead of me.*
*Thanks for the good time last night.*
*Breakfast is on me.*
*Jesse*

I quietly slipped out the door, climbed into my pickup truck, and headed west.

## CHAPTER 9 – Wall Art

### *Niki*

"Do you like it?" Kat's eyes were beaming, when she showed me her rather abstract paint job on the wall in her room.

*So much for getting our security deposit back when we move out.*

"It's…um…interesting. Very artistic," I replied.

"I knew you would like it," she said hugging me. "I'm so happy we finally did this. We are going to have so much fun."

"We sure will. Careful, hon, don't get paint all over me. This is a brand new shirt."

"Aww, you are such a wimp. It's just a little paint. It will wash off." She laughed and reached for the brush. Oh, I knew exactly what she was up to and ran for the door, barely escaping being part of her artwork. I slammed it shut, held it tight, and trapped her inside.

"Hey, let me out," Kat yelled, rattling the doorknob.

"Only if you promise to put down the brush." I was trying not to laugh.

"Okay, okay. I promise," she giggled.

"Pinky swear?"

"Geez, what are we, in high school? Okay, I pinky swear. Now, let me out."

I released my hold on the knob and Kat opened the door with a swoosh. She stood in the doorway, cheeks flushed red, still holding the paintbrush. "Hey, you promised," I reminded her.

Kat hesitated for a brief moment but decided to comply. "Let's go for lunch," she said as she dropped the brush in the sink and pulled the paint-stained T-shirt over her head. "Give me half an hour. I'm just gonna take a quick shower and then we can leave, okay?"

I could see a pattern emerging. She would leave the mess for me to clean up. Not a great start.

*~*~*

Café Vida in the Palisades was bustling with patrons. After a short five-minute wait, Kat and I were sitting comfortably in a small booth.

The waitress placed a basket of freshly baked bread between us. Kat broke off a piece to chew on while talking. "Now that you've moved away from your dad's iron-tight grip, I hope you'll finally say goodbye to that stuffy boyfriend of yours."

"You never liked Jason, did you?"

"Damn right. You need a new man."

I pulled a piece from the same crusty loaf of

sourdough. "What's so wrong with Jason? He's what every girl wants. Smart, has a good job, a good future…"

"And boring. Niki, the guy's lifeless. You need a cool and fun guy. If you want, I can help you find a new one. Trust me, I'm good at this."

"I don't want a new guy. Funny, cool or not. I'm perfectly happy right now."

"So are you?"

"Am I what? Happy? I just told you I am." I set down the bread that I had been nibbling.

"No, silly, are you gonna end it with Jason anytime soon?"

"I already told you. This is not the right time in my life for any breakups. They're too emotional. Why do you even care so much?"

"Because I have exciting plans for us this summer and we don't want some dreary tagalong, like Jason."

"Hah, it's not such an easy thing to do. You know, it is not just one person getting hurt here. In fact, I am not even sure who will be most affected, Jason or my dad."

Kat cracked a smile. "Your dad had it all figured out, didn't he? Hooking you up with Daddy's golden boy at the office. Together they can draw out the rest of your life for you. Listen, Niki, this is your time. Your destiny. Nobody but you should dictate how you should live. It is not freaking India, where women are forced into arranged marriages."

"Wow, that would be scary. At least now I am out of the house. Away from my dad's constant disapproving scorn. But Jason is a nice solid guy. Everyone says we're perfect for each other."

"Yeah, well. Perfect doesn't always cut it. Wait and see."

I frowned and stabbed a forkful of the salad that the waitress had delivered to our table. Kat had a way of being right about people, an instinctive kind of understanding. I didn't want to admit that she was right. Again. But I just didn't have time to deal with relationship issues right now so I changed the subject.

"Are we still on for going out Saturday night in Venice Beach?"

"Definitely. Party time is on, my friend. Chase, Tanner, and Jenna are going too. V Lounge will be a blast. The last time I was there, it was filled with hot guys. It was like they were hanging off the wall fixtures, there were so many. Could be our lucky night."

"Ha." I laughed and nearly choked on a piece of lettuce. "Kat, you're crazy, girl. You always see the positive in things. But I'm sure if there are tons of hunky guys they will all be after you. That's why I keep you around, you are always so much fun to be with."

Kat laughed and took a sip of her drink. "So I hope you are not bringing Mr. Killjoy with you on Saturday to the V Lounge?"

"Actually, you are in luck. He'll be out of town.

We had a big fight about it. His family planned a big celebration for his grandmother's eightieth birthday. He assumed I would go with him but it's all the way up past San Francisco. That's a seven-hour drive each way. I can't waste my entire weekend. I need to finish a big fashion design project that's due next week. So I argued like the lawyer my dad wants me to be. And he argued like the lawyer he is and the whole thing blew up into a big mess. But I stood my ground in the end."

"Good for you, Niki, way to stand up for yourself."

"I feel guilty for not playing the role of the supportive girlfriend, but I would have felt so out of place with all of his family there. I have hardly met any of them except his parents, once. I don't think our relationship is ready for that big of an event yet. Maybe if we were a year or two into our relationship, but not now. You know what I mean."

"Sure, hon. Now we can have some fun together this Saturday." Kat finished the last bite of her salad and pulled out her wallet from her oversized Juicy Couture bag.

## CHAPTER 10 - Rookies

*Jesse*

"Hope this will work for you," Kenny said, opening the door to the spare bedroom in his house.

"This is great. Thanks, Ken." I dropped my suitcase on the floor next to the bed. It was a cool place Uncle Kenny had. Right in the heart of Santa Monica, only a few blocks from the beach. A typical California-style house that looked like all the others on the block—light colors, stucco exterior. East Coast houses were different. Darker and more rustic than on the West Coast. Not a lot of red brick houses in LA.

I stepped over to the window and pushed the vertical blinds aside with the back side of my hand to check out the view. *Damn.* Bigger yards in New York too, I noted as I surveyed the patio area. But what the hell, the sun was shining and the room was bright, painted all white. I scanned it from ceiling to floor. This would be my home away from home for the next couple months.

Shit, who was I kidding; I didn't have a home. I'd been crashing at Jimmy's place in between races, ever since Mom went in the hospital and our old house was sold to help pay her medical bills. But I had a good feeling about this visit. Spending the summer here, helping my uncle to get "Rookies," his sports bar, off the ground might not be such a bad idea after all.

"Help yourself to anything you need. Towels, bedding, and stuff. There's plenty of food and beer in the fridge. Mi casa es su casa." He cracked a feeble smile. I hadn't seen him for years and wrinkles had settled around his eyes. And yet, for his age of forty-five, he wasn't a bad looking dude and stayed in good shape, it seemed. I always wondered why he never married, or had any kids. He had a good heart, fun and easy-going, one of those guys everyone gets along with. I guess that's why he opened his bar. Kenny was your typical friendly bartender.

"Thanks again. I really appreciate it. Just let me know what you need from me. I'm here to help, you know."

"Sure, Jess, no problem. Take a day or two and get settled in. I'll take you to the bar Monday and show you around. It'll be the easiest job you've ever had," Kenny said with a smile, and paused as he went out the door. "Oh, but don't walk around the house naked. I'm having female company later, if you know what I mean."

"Uncle Kenny." I grinned. "You dog, you."

Kenny disappeared down the hall, whistling, and I headed out to the truck to get the remainder of my bags.

*~*~*

"Jess, meet Chase. He is my right hand here at the bar. Been with me ever since I opened this joint. Chase, this is my nephew, Jesse Morrison from New York."

Chase stuck out his hand. "Hey, man. Great to meet you. Kenny told me you were coming out here to help with the bar over the summer."

It was Monday morning and my uncle had brought me to his sports bar, "Rookies," to get me acclimated. It was my first day helping out and I was feeling pretty chill about the whole thing. Hanging around bars was not exactly new to me.

I shook Chase's hand. He had a firm grip, was well-built, and seemed like a nice guy. "Great to meet you too, man. Yep, I'm out here for a couple of months, I guess. We'll see how it goes."

"Chase will show you around and explain the routine. Train you for the job." We stepped into the back hallway near his office. "Chase, will you get Jesse his uniform?"

I cringed at the word "uniform." I wasn't a military "everyone wear the same outfit" type of guy. Chase nodded in affirmation.

"I thought you were going to train me yourself, Uncle Kenny?"

It was Kenny's turn to cringe. He wrinkled his face. "You're going to have to drop the 'uncle' thing. It sounds so...old. And just not right for our working situation."

"Sure, sure. Kenny. You got it...Boss."

Kenny clapped me on my cheek as if he were some godfather out of the old Mafia movies. "Well, better get your thumb out of your ass and get to work." He turned to Chase.

"Chase, I'll be in my office for the next couple hours if you need me." He took a step towards his office and stopped to pull his wallet out of his pocket, handing Chase a couple bills. "Lunch is on me since its Jesse's first day, but after that you two knuckleheads are on your own. Don't drink it all up—get some food, too. And call me if you need anything." He turned to me. "Jess, I'll see you later." He slapped me on the back and gave a nod to Chase. "Have fun, guys." He disappeared into his office down the hall and left me standing there facing Chase.

"Your uncle is a pretty cool dude. Come on. I'll give you the tour."

I followed him out to the bar area. "Yeah, he's always been solid. It's good to see him again after all these years."

"What do you mean? How long has it been since you two have seen each other?"

"God, I don't know, lost count. The last five years I've been on nonstop tours racing Motocross and

Supercross. I'm hardly in one place for very long, well, until this damn injury." I raised my left hand and opened and closed my fist. "I haven't gained back the strength I need for the proper grip and control of the bike."

"Shit, that sucks. I could help you work on that, you know, target those muscles with some strength training. I'm also a trainer at a gym here in Santa Monica."

"Maybe. Tell me. What's up with the uniform thing? I didn't know I was gonna be wearing some lame-ass uniform. I can't be messing with my swag, you know?"

Chase laughed and shook his head. "Don't sweat the load, man. It's just a polo shirt with the 'Rookies' logo. Nothing elaborate. See, I'm wearing it. Sometimes red, sometimes a black shirt." He pulled on the collar.

"Yeah, you look kind of geeky." I grinned. Chase knew I was yanking his chain and I could tell right away he was my kind of guy. This gig was going to be a fucking piece of cake.

The rest of the morning was spent in training. Chase showed me the basics needed to tend bar. He also hooked me up with the goofy polo shirt-slash-uniform and finally we headed to a Chipotle on my uncle's dime. About time—my stomach was starting to roar.

"Tell me, Jess," Chase said, downing a large bite of his burrito. "California is a long way from New York. A long way to travel for a summer gig. Anything else bring you to the West Coast, besides your uncle?"

"Basically, I'm an asshole and needed a change of

scenery." I wasn't going to lie and try to pretty myself up for anyone. I am what I am.

"Dude, that's kind of a rough description of yourself. Man, what did you do to earn that title?" Chase asked with a grin.

"It's a long story but the shorter version is, I was at the peak of my racing career and, like I told you earlier, I messed up my hand and my leg." I dropped my taco and wiggled the fingers of my left hand in the air. "The surgery on my hand didn't take right, my grip's fucked up now. If I can't clasp the handlebar and work the clutch with my hand like I used to, I'm screwed. I may never race professionally again."

"Man, that sucks. Where did you race?"

"All over the states, Australia, and even in Europe. Last year I won Supercross du Paris in France."

"No kidding. Wow! You must have been pretty skilled on a bike. I'm impressed."

"After my accident, things just went south. I couldn't ride the way I used to and that killed me. I need to ride. It's ingrained in my pores, my blood. I crave that kind of action in my life, it fuels my soul. What the hell am I gonna do without it?" I shrugged and crunched into more taco. "Don't have any other job skills. Spent all my life on a dirt bike, never even went to college. Don't get me wrong, college is fine for...someone else. But me? Nah, I need the adrenaline rush every day. I would die if I had to get a job like sitting behind a desk all day. Literally die. I'd rather just take a gun to my head and get it over with fast, than spend the rest of my life at a desk job. Suicide by desk, I call it." I cracked a smile, leaned back in my chair, crumpled the taco paper into a ball and tossed it onto the brown plastic tray. "So, I became an asshole instead. Drinking, whoring, and partying. Anything to fill the void, getting my rush in a different way. Oh, and then there was this whole thing about my brother, Jimmy. He's a cop. His career, wife and future kid didn't mesh well with my lifestyle. After he pulled me out of yet another bar fight, he 'suggested' I leave town and chill out here with Uncle Kenny for a while. Get my shit in one bag, you know. And basically, that's why I'm here."

Chase pushed his tray away and crossed his arms across his chest. "That's quite a story. Well, I guess we all have one, but no worries, man. I'm not here to judge."

"That's cool."

"And Jess, don't worry about your hand. The human body is a pretty remarkable piece of equipment. I think I can help you with that hand. Don't give up just yet, man. Let's see what we can do. I'll design a specific training plan for you. I can't promise anything but I might have a trick or two up my sleeve."

"I doubt anything will work. I went to all of my physical therapy sessions after the surgery and it still looks like shit. I think I'm just destined to be an asshole." I laughed, ran my hand through my hair, and sucked down the rest of my Coke.

"We'd better beat it. It's time to go back." Chase stood up from the table and tipped his tray of trash into the can. He put the plastic tray up on top near the soda station and we shoved off into the bright California sunshine. I wasn't used to walking to lunch or walking to work back in New York, it was a new experience for me. It kind of made me feel like I was cheating on my truck.

The early afternoon hours were spent with more training—how to replace the beer kegs when they run empty, how to operate the glass-washing station, how to prepare the set-ups for mixed drinks, and where to find all the bar supplies. Tonight, I would be the bartender's assistant, helping Chase with anything he needed. Chase would train me in how to mix drinks and be an expert bartender later in the week. It was pretty easy stuff and I got a chance to get my feet wet, drawing beers from the tap for the after-work customers.

A couple of days had gone by and I considered myself almost an expert, filling the heavy glass beer mugs with just the right head of foam. Every night I waited for "the big rush" of customers, but the reality was that my uncle's bar was more like a graveyard. I wondered if my stay at my uncle's house would be shorter-lived than I had anticipated.

Saturday rolled around and I'd been in California for almost a week, working my butt off day and night at "Rookies." All I'd seen was the dark inside of the bar, and my bed, for too long. I was restless and needed to blow off some steam. Hell, I didn't even know what Santa Monica looked like in the daylight, but Chase came through with an invite to a bar. Hang with him and some of his friends.

Chase was texting when I slid into the passenger seat of his car.

"Hey, man." His eyes were glued to the screen. He finished his text, dropped the phone in the console cup holder, and put the car in reverse. "Are you ready for this? Santa Monica nightlife?"

"Hell, yeah." I pushed my hand through my hair.

"Tonight you can see how we rock things here on the West Coast."

"Where're we going?"

"V Lounge. Some friends of mine from back in high school said to meet up there. That's who I was texting. I haven't seen them for a while but they are chill and fun."

"Cool. I'm down."

As we headed to Venice Beach my mind was set on the burn of a Jack Daniels. New surroundings and a change to my daily grind had kept my mind off my own crap—most of the time. But my injured hand kept me constantly pissed off and reminded me of the calming effect hard liquor induced.

As we entered the V Lounge, Chase quickly noticed his group of friends. "There they are, in the corner over there." He pointed with his chin to a small group with a hot blonde, reaching up on her tiptoes, frantically waving at us. We pushed through the mass of warm bodies in their direction. I swept the room with my eyes. Drinks were flowing like water all around us. I liked this place. I liked it a lot.

"Chase," she squealed. The hot blonde threw her arms around Chase's neck bouncing up and down. *Damn, I would like to see that bouncing action riding me.*

"Whoa, whoa, Kat. Take it easy on my neck, girl." He laughed. "Glad to see me, or what?"

The girl giggled and tossed back her long blonde hair. "Chase sweetie, who's your friend here?" She radiated as she turned to scope me out, one arm thrown over Chase's shoulder and a seductive glitter in her eye. She'd been drinking already. Always an attractive quality in my book. I pushed my hand through my hair, feeling like a side of beef hanging in a meat market.

"Kat, this is Jesse, he's the newbie at Rookies. He's Kenny's nephew," Chase said.

She dropped her arm from his neck and gawked at me hungrily. I could really go for this chick. Hot piece of ass. The kind of girl who'd play into my lifestyle nicely.

"Hey, Jesse. Where've you been all my life?" She turned back to the bar and grabbed her cranberry vodka.

"Are you a fitness trainer or something? You're pretty damn hot with all those muscles and shit." She gazed up at me from under her lashes, like she could jump on me and eat me alive. Damn, this girl could sure turn the tables. Suddenly the hunter became the hunted. I liked it. Easier for me to be a player.

I shuffled my feet. "Well, what can I say? I'm vegetarian and hit the gym religiously." I was being sarcastic. She didn't get it.

"Really?" she asked with wide eyes.

Chase blew out a sudden short laugh.

"No. Are you whack? My idea of weightlifting is lifting beer bottles to my lips," I snorted.

She stomped her foot and huffed. "You guys suck ass."

I eyed the bartender behind her, anxious to get a drink in me to better deal with this little vixen.

"Hey, Jesse hon. C'mon, you gotta meet my best friend." Before I knew it she was pulling on my arm for me to follow her a couple spots down the bar. When we stopped, my eyes lingered on a girl with long dark hair, in an outrageously short black dress, standing at the bar with her back to us.

"Niki!"

The girl heard her name and turned with a drink in hand, long black locks undulating down her back in a wave as she moved. My eyes beaded a line straight on her face, fair and sweet, that imprinted on my soul in a heartbeat. I swore I heard the buzz of electricity, and for a nanosecond time froze. My awareness of the room momentarily faded into a hazy blur, followed by another cool glance over her shoulder. And with that, the room warped back to normal.

Kat tugged on her friend's arm, pulling her attention away from some dude who had been chewing her ear off.

"Niki. You gotta meet Jesse. He's Chase's new friend and coworker. Kenny's nephew."

The sweet-faced girl turned completely around, looking right into me like she could see through me, like she could see all the way to where my thoughts originated. How I had never minded wasting my life on cheap beer…or cheap women.

"Jesse, this is my best friend in the whole world, Niki. We've known each other since high school, well, all of us have. Anyway…oh my God, I think I need another drink," Kat said to the bottom of her empty glass.

"Hi, Jesse, nice to meet you," Niki said. Her lush lips moved. Her dark lashes batted. Her reaction towards me was pleasant, but she didn't look impressed. My heart sank. Holy hell, I just met this girl and already the sparks were flying like heat lightning arcing between storm clouds. At least that was my reaction. *Fuck.* This was unusual for me. None of my usual bar whores and one-night stands ever caused this kind of reaction.

Her eyes flitted over to Chase and lit up with old

friendship when she saw him.

"Chase, baby, good to see you again." She leaned past me to give Chase a hug. A wisp of her raven hair brushed my arm. "Chase, where've you been hiding? I haven't seen you around lately." Her scent pleasantly invaded my nostrils. My pulse jabbed at my veins, with a sharp burst of adrenaline.

*Damn, that felt good.*

"Chase, dude, I need a drink," I said. "Let's flag down the bartender." Chase pressed into the bodies closest to the edge of the bar and waved. He shouted our order over their heads and I shoved a twenty-dollar bill at him to pay for our drinks.

Niki stood to my rear, wedged in between me and Chase, almost pressed up against his chest, the crowd was so tight. Even at that close range, their conversation was strained and she had to yell to be heard over the music and bar chatter. This arrangement left me trapped on the receiving end of Kat's nuclear attention, her off-the-wall personality oozing enthusiasm in my face.

"Jesse, you look dark and mysterious to me. Where are you from again? New Hampshire?"

She practically scaled me like Mount Everest when Chase passed over my drink, holding it high above all the heads. Too many people. It sloshed in the glass and dribbled on Kat's bare forearm, causing her to squeal.

"Oh, shit, that's cold." She laughed, shaking imaginary drops off her arm.

"Sorry, didn't mean to baptize you with beer."

She kept laughing. "It's okay, Jesse. You can lick it off." She held her arm up to my face and laughed loudly. "Just kidding, lover. You can do it later," she giggled.

This chick was hot and all, the total package, but damn, she just wasn't tripping my trigger anymore. Niki had lit a spark in me that baffled me. How could one look be so powerful? I shot a glance back over my shoulder. Niki was still at my back, deep in a conversation with Chase. I could hear snippets of conversation fading in and out, the two of them rehashing old high school memories. Damn, if I knew her in high school I never would have let that one get away. Secret tingles amassed on my skin, knowing how dangerously close she was behind me. Was it the heat from her body, or heat from the conglomerate of human flesh? *Shit*. What was happening to me? I downed the rest of my beer and ordered another.

"Okay, Jesse, let's play a game."

Oh my God, no. Let's not play a fucking guessing game. I blew out a breath, twisted around a little to check on Niki. Still hanging on Chase.

"So, Jesse, huh? What do you think? What's your answer? Mary Ann or Ginger?" Kat was all up in my face. I had no clue what the fuck she was talking about. I hadn't even heard a word she said.

"Uh, well…" I noticed a couple leaving. "There's a table. Let's snag it before anyone else gets it." I lurched through the crowd to a round high-top table and staked a claim with my beer glass.

I yelled back, "Chase, Niki, I got a table over here."

The wooden leg of the tall chair groaned against the cement floor as I pulled it out for Niki. Kat jumped into the chair. "Thanks, hon."

I looked up and Chase caught the pained expression on my face. He slid into the chair next to Kat to run interference for me.

# CHAPTER 11 – V Lounge

## *Niki*

Kat dipped her head into mine. "Isn't he cute?" she said, laying claim to Jesse. It was a familiar scenario; Kat drew all the attention when we went out. I glanced over the sleek black tabletop, hoping Jesse wouldn't catch me looking. It was obvious he was interested in Kat, yet he intrigued me. He looked down into his beer, laughing at something Kat said. I tried hard not to notice anything about him. It would be best to ignore him. He was probably a "player," nothing but trouble. But the minute we met my eyes discerned several things: his dark blue eyes, the way stray locks of hair fell in his eyes and how he pushed them back, his charming smile, his ink, and a pack of muscles that moved powerfully under his tight gray T-shirt. But I shouldn't have noticed. I already had a boyfriend.

"Yeah, he's hot as hell." I took a sip of beer and vowed to divert my thoughts from Jesse. Chase and Jesse had ordered a pitcher and we all shared. It was good to see Chase again. We almost dated in high school, but it was awkward. Sometimes friends are meant to stay as friends. Maybe if he had been as good-looking back then as now, it would've been different. It took some time for him to ripen. Now he was definitely handsome, tall, and muscular, with jet-black hair that was cut short in the back and longer in the front.

"Well, hands off, Niki girl. I'm claiming 'new guy in town' for myself."

"Kat, you're a crazy woman. I have Jason, remember?" I played it off like I hadn't been the least bit affected by Jesse. Yeah, I had Jason. With that thought, my eyes flashed over to Jesse again and my heart wilted.

Jason was very literal-minded, no understanding of music or poetry, and yet when you got right down to it, Jason's literalness, his pragmatic approach to every subject, was the primary reason he was cut out to be a lawyer, and it made him invulnerable. He was smart, even-tempered, and…and rather flat, and boring. That was it, it plain and clear, and as usual, Kat was spot-on.

Tonight, restlessness rumbled in my gut, stoked by the staleness of my relationship with Jason. I'd made a lot of changes in my life lately and each gave more power to the next, a domino effect. It was no wonder I was on edge. Or maybe Jesse was just damn hot. And he got my head all turned around.

"Fuck that shit, Niki. Jason is a dickhead. Dump him, you deserve so much better." She took a swig of her beer, as if to give credence to her words. The edge to her words was all a facade and I never took offense. Kat could read people in an instant. She picked up on Jason's control issue long before I did and aired her opinion right from the get-go.

"What the hell do you mean, Kat?" The beers had absorbed straight into my bloodstream and I giggled. "Jason is the pitomee…" My tongue had a mind of its own inside my mouth. "Jason is the e-pit-omy of a good boyfriend." I leaned in heavily onto the table, touching heads with Kat as we laughed.

"Girl, I love you. You're the best roommate ever." Kat flung an arm over my shoulder and rubbed her head against mine and kissed me on the cheek. Jesse leaned over, invading our space, and I raised my head to a pair of solid blue eyes burning a hole in me. Once again, his unruly strands of brown hair fell into his eyes. He shoved them back with his hand. It drew my attention to the movement of muscles under his inked skin. Entirely unaware of it, Jesse knew how to push all my buttons. My blood simmered. My eyelashes fluttered. I pulled back, shoving my drink in my mouth to cover the gasp I surely made. *Oh shit.* Jason was out of town for his grandmother's birthday, and here I was lusting after the first hot guy who crossed my path. What was wrong with me?

"Can I join the party? You two are pretty tight over here." Playfully, he nudged my elbow and a shiver ran up my arm. "Can a new guy get a word in?"

"Oh sorry, baby." Kat said. "Come in here and join

us."

Chase must have gone to the restroom, as I couldn't see him anywhere in the crowd. Jesse was breathing down my neck. Every second near him was like resisting a powerful electromagnet. I needed Chase back at the table to divert my attention before the alcohol made me do something stupid. Kat pulled her arm off me and draped it over Jesse's broad, muscular shoulder.

"Damn, baby. You work out." Kat slurred, running her forefinger up and down his bulging bicep. It traced across the edge of a tattoo peeking out from under the tight sleeve of his T-shirt. I cocked my head to the side and read, "Carpe Diem." A slight tug pulled in the pit of my stomach, as I allowed my eyes to vacation on his powerful ink-covered muscles. I whimpered in my mind, and bit my tongue, while I watched Kat soak up all the testosterone-laden attention at the table. I closed my eyes and gulped my beer.

*Jason, Jason, Jason. Remember Jason.*

At least I had drab thoughts of "boring old Jason" to squelch the fire Jesse started in me. I exhaled and relaxed as Kat and Jesse focused on each other. I drummed my fingers, waiting for Chase. Kat was falling all over Jesse and I wouldn't be surprised if she took him home with her, or she went home with him.

*Damn it, Kat, cool your jets. We're roommates.*

I didn't want to see her with him, or *hear* her with him at our place later tonight. I could crash on Chase's couch if things headed in that direction.

"Who's ready for some shots?" Chase sang out, returning to the table with four shots of Patron. "Yeah. I'm ready."

"Hell, yeah. I know I am," Jesse's voice joined in.

Chase put them down and high-fived Jesse. Kat doled out the shots, one in front of each of us, a lime wedge teetering on the edge of each glass. Chase held his up, signaling everyone to raise a glass in unison. "Here's to old friends and new."

He threw back his shot and we all followed suit. I coughed and sputtered, feeling the burn in my throat. I was never much of an expert at shots. Sipping wine was more my style, but as we toasted, I noted that Jesse appeared to be quite the pro at chugging drinks. With the back of my hand, I wiped lime juice from my mouth and mentally chastised myself. Who was I kidding? Jesse's demeanor had "bad boy" written all over it, as one who could hook up with a girl in no time flat. Normally I wouldn't give a guy like that the time of day and yet his eyes had pierced me to my soul, awakening something in me that I hadn't realized existed. And he pushed into my mind more often than I wanted to admit.

Corralled at the table by friends the remainder of the night, I was a reluctant witness to Kat's well-crafted play for Mr. Bad Boy himself. I chewed the thin short drink straw in my empty glass to shreds. I knew he would break her heart like a typical bad boy. Just another troublemaker. Run, Kat, hightail it outta here. I sank my teeth into my lower lip, reached for the glass. Chase had just sat down and swallowed a huge gulp of beer.

"Hey, Niki, that was mine." Chase blinked at me, like he was hurt, and plopped down in the chair next to mine. Kat and Jesse were practically conjoined twins by now, locked into a fascinating conversation, garnished with lots of high-pitched laughing and hair-tossing. I wanted to puke. Well, maybe it was the alcohol that made me want to puke.

"Yeah, whatever, I need this to drown my sorrows." I leaned heavily on the tabletop, loose as a rag doll, and verbally vomited all the drama of the Jason situation onto Chase. He was a sympathetic listener, so I heaved a second time, and the story about my dad and moving out to find my freedom came spilling out. Such are the effects of mixing your liquors: beer, vodka, and tequila.

"Come on, girl." A strong hand reached over, taking me by the elbow. I looked up with blurry vision into Jesse's heavenly blue eyes. "Come on, you. It's time to go home."

"Niki, I think we need to go now, hon," Kat slurred, and swayed while grabbing the back of my chair to steady herself.

"Where are we going? I don't want to go home yet," I blubbered.

They both snickered at how poorly Kat and I held our liquor. Jesse tugged on my arm a second time, but I yanked it away.

"Nah. I think I'll stay and have one more." I shifted in my chair like I was settling in.

"Hey, come on, Niki. It's time to get out of here. I'll get you ladies in a cab and send you home," Chase said. "Both of you two need to call it a night."

He gently put his hands on my waist and moved me out of the chair. I struggled to stand, finding everything, and nothing in particular, hilarious.

"Niki-i-i-i. Come on. Woo…" Kat whooped and flung her arm over my shoulder. The force was enough to make me fall into Jesse, standing next to us. I grabbed at his T-shirt, laughing, and Kat's petite body followed, the two of us crashing into him like falling dominoes.

"Woo, hoo!" Kat yelped. "Let's make a sandwich." She wrapped her arms around me, reaching all the way to Jesse, for one big hug. Spontaneously, he circled his arms around the both of us in a "sandwich hug.". I found myself caught in the middle, pressed up against a solid pack of muscles. Even in my inebriated state, his lethal energy radiated through me and I melted into his chest. I tipped my head back, looking up at him, my mouth hanging open. And there I froze, painfully aware of how awkward the situation was, wondering if he· could feel my heart beating against his chest. Oh God, he probably thought I was falling all over him like all the other girls.

*Damn you, drunken Kat.*

Kat was oblivious, lost in her own world, dancing to one big party inside her head—jostling me up and down, locked in the middle of some kind of crazy, psychotic bear hug, pumping to the bar music.

"Wooo! Let's da-a-nce," Kat squealed.

*Oh my God, just let me die now.*

"The party is over, Kat," Chase chuckled. "Come on. Let's get out of this place before you start dancing on the tables." He tugged at her arm and she let go of the hug, releasing me from my blissful torture session.

"Oh, that's a good idea. I could do that. Maybe I'd get a few dollar bills…"

"No, no, no, no," He steered her back towards the exit.

"This way. To the door, party girl. We're not in Vegas."

I lurched for Chase's arm. I would only be tempting fate if I stayed within Jesse's personal bubble. And to no surprise, Kat latched herself onto Jesse's arm.

Outside on the curb, the summer night air was fresh on my face. A dirty cab pulled up in front of us.

"Here's your limo, girls," Jesse said.

"What? We don't need a cab," Kat protested.

Chase pulled her arm. "You're insane. There's no way in hell you can drive tonight, Kat. Jesse called you girls a cab."

"That's right, get in, Cinderella. Your pumpkin has arrived," Jesse said, and opened the door of the cab.

"Hey, maybe you can take me home," Kat said,

pulling closer to Jesse.

"Sorry, not tonight, sugar," Jesse said, as he escorted her to the open car door. He pushed her into the back seat of the cab, a petite mass of flesh babbling and laughing. She fell back giggling, the cab driver cutting her an annoyed glance. Jesse apologized to the man and took her legs by the ankles, shoving them in after her, like he was stuffing an oversized duffle bag.

Jesse now turned, one hand still on the door, and held out his other hand for me. I stood, wide-eyed, staring. Oh, shit. My heart did a flipflop. I knew he was simply being polite, but he had no idea what havoc his presence had wreaked upon me. My eyes flitted from his open waiting hand up to his face. His stare cut through me, as he smiled a charming smile, causing my stomach to tie itself in knots. I swallowed hard and put my hand in his, trying not to come undone. Maybe I had been wrong about him. Maybe he wasn't a player after all.

I dropped down into the seat, as he shut the door and stepped back away from the cab. Chase thumped the top of the car with his hand and walked off. Jesse shoved his hands in his pockets and walked backwards, bent over, looking down to see me peering out the window, as the cab pulled away from the curb. I jerked my face from the window, embarrassed that he caught me gawking. I could've sworn I saw him blow me a two-fingered kiss. I gasped and spun around to see if Kat had witnessed it.

"Kat!" She was silent, slumped back in the seat with her eyes closed and her mouth open.

I audibly exhaled and relaxed back into the seat, and Kat's soft elbow fell against my arm. She would sleep it off and wake with a pounding headache in the morning. What the fuck had happened tonight? Kat was going after Jesse pretty hard, yet I repeatedly caught him staring at me. And the electrifying vibes between us were off the charts. My eyes blankly focused out the cab window the rest of the ride home, unaware of the cityscape rushing past. There were some things in life that couldn't be explained, but I had a quirky feeling Hurricane Jesse was about to hit land.

# CHAPTER 12 – No Pain No Gain

## *Jesse*

"C'mon, Chase, give me her number," I pleaded. I worked my left hand, doing curls with a hand weight. Chase was helping me strengthen the muscles in my injured hand at the gym where he worked part-time as a trainer.

"I'm not giving you Niki's number, dude. I know you, you'll just fuck her over with a one-night stand, and I don't want her hurt. Niki and I have been friends since high school."

I couldn't believe he was cock-blocking me like this. Maybe the real reason he refused to give me her number was that he was into Niki himself. "Seriously, dude, I'm not like that. That was the old me. I just want to take her on a date and see how it goes. You know, two people getting to know each other like adults."

"Jesse," he stopped and stared straight at me. "You are only here for the summer, man. Suppose you two hit it off? Then what? You leave and I have to put up with tears and all the, 'What did I do wrong?' whining and crying, and help her get over you. I don't know. It doesn't sound like a good idea. Besides, she has a boyfriend, well, a kind of boyfriend. I don't really know how serious they are, but still, you gotta think about that."

Fuck. A boyfriend? That explained why she was a little cold at first. Did it really matter? It's not like they were married or anything. And what if it was just something casual? Chase had no idea how my heart skyrocketed when she turned around and I saw her face for the first time. It was like a fucking beautiful heart attack in a little black dress. Something inside of me burst to life. It was like an instant addiction to a drug and it was all her, those big doe eyes, her long dark hair. Fuck! It was better than XTC and coke combined. It scared the shit out of me to admit it, but I was hooked. Boyfriend or no boyfriend, I was going all in. And I could be a pretty damn persistent asshole if needed.

"You're killing me here, man. Just give me the number. Besides, if you don't, I'll just get it from Kat." I raised my eyebrows.

Chase rolled his eyes. "Will you forget about Niki, already? I have another idea. Some friends and I are going to a private beach in Malibu for a bonfire tonight. There'll be plenty of good-looking girls with slamming hot bodies. You can come with me."

Damn. I didn't care about slamming hot bodies. I could get that anywhere. I had to figure out why this Niki girl had such an effect on me. I finished my reps with the hand weights while contemplating a way to get to see her again.

"What if you called Kat and Niki and invited them to that bonfire thing?" I asked, but I had lost Chase's attention.

"Well, speak of the devil." Chase pointed towards the elliptical machines with his chin as he alternated forearm curls. Niki and Kat were talking and climbing onto the machines. The moment my eyes gazed upon Niki, my pulse jumped. She looked even hotter than I remembered. Oh shit, another quake on the Richter scale. So it wasn't just my imagination last night, or the effects of the damn beer.

I never had much faith in love. For me, love had always been more about physical release than anything else, but when I saw Niki, something was different. My heart skipped a beat and I felt driven to be with her by some unexplainable force. I knew I would pursue her with everything I had, even if she had some loser boyfriend. I had to give it a shot. I couldn't deny the emotions churning inside and my instincts told me she felt it too.

Chase furrowed his brow. "I've never seen them at my gym before."

I chuckled. "I 'accidentally' told Kat last night we were gonna train here today. I'll go talk to them."

"What? You're a sneaky bastard, my friend."

I headed over to the row of elliptical machines. I didn't have a game plan. I just knew I had to talk to

Niki.

"Well, look who's here. I can't believe you two have the energy to work out after last night."

Kat gave me a big smile, but my eyes were on Niki's face, checking to see what kind of reaction she would give me.

"Hey, Jesse," Kat chirped, working her arms and legs on the machine. "Gotta work the toxins out of our systems. Sweat them out. Burn off that hangover.

"Good for you. I usually keep going...you know, keep drinking the next day, but that'll work too." My eyes burned holes through Niki. *God, stop it! I'm gonna scare her off.*

"Did you have a good time last night?" Niki asked.

"Yeah, very cool. You ladies sure know how to party."

Niki wiped a bead of sweat from her forehead. She looked ravishing. "Yeah, last night was fun, except I think I had one too many. Tequila shots hit me hard." Niki threw me one of her beautiful, full-lipped smiles, and my heart did that thing again, a little flip. I didn't want to offend her by staring at her body, but it was exquisite. Her tight-fitting exercise clothes defined every voluptuous bulge and curve.

"Trust me. You're not alone in that department." My gaze wandered to Kat and I shot her a crooked smile.

"What?" Kat interrupted. "Are you insinuating I can't hold my liquor?

"I said no such thing," I lied. "I'm sure you can

drink me under the table any day of the week."

"Oh God, let's not go there." Niki laughed and Kat rolled her eyes.

"So listen," I said. "I gotta get back to my workout. But how about you two meet up with Chase and me down at the beach tonight for a bonfire?"

Niki opened her mouth to speak but Kat answered for her, "Awesome." She got down from her elliptical machine and placed one hand on my triceps, rubbing it. "It's gotta be more than beer bottles you lift to get this toned, Jesse. I can't wait for tonight."

Kat's flirtations were becoming an annoyance, like a pesky fly. Just like last night, I hardly had a chance to talk to Niki and I wanted to know everything about her. I wanted to pull her long dark hair out of that twitching ponytail and watch it curl down over her bare shoulders.

It was pretty obvious that Kat wanted to hook, and normally I would've gone all the way with a girl like her. But not last night. Last night it was all Niki on my mind. I couldn't take my fucking eyes off her. I didn't want to mess up my chances with Niki by getting drunk and being tempted to do something stupid with her best friend, Kat. A one-night stand with her roommate would've fucked up any chance of getting closer to Niki. That's why I called a cab for them. For once, I didn't want a girl for her tits and ass...who the fuck was I kidding, I always wanted tits and ass. But there was more than that about Niki. Something special. I couldn't pinpoint it, a kind of gentleness in her eyes. Last night, I knew right then and there, I had to have her. The stupid old cliché "struck by lightning" made perfect sense. The only bump in the road would be to convince her to ditch that damn boyfriend of hers.

"Text me the location later. Is the bonfire here in Santa Monica?" Kat asked.

"No, actually, it's a private beach at Malibu," I answered Kat but my eyes focused on Niki.

"Well, whatever, just text me where it's at," Kat said.

"Sure. And Niki…"

She stopped her movement on the machine and turned to me. "What?"

"I'll see you tonight," I said with a smile. My heart skipped as Niki smiled back. *Shit!* I was like a fucking teenage kid with his first crush.

Without missing a beat, Kat interrupted with nonstop chatter,. "Later, Jesse. Text me. Can't wait. This is going to be awesome. I'm stoked for a bonfire. How about you, Niki? I haven't been to a bonfire in ages, no wait, I think we went last fall with, oh, what's his name, you know…"

I walked away grinning from ear to ear, as Kat's chatter faded into the background noise of the gym.

# CHAPTER 13 – Bon Fire

## *Niki*

"Niki, will you grab my guitar?"

"I've already got the cooler and chips. I can't carry everything."

Kat sighed, opened the back car door of her Prius, and grabbed a tote bag, guitar case, and a folding beach chair. We left the car in the paid parking lot near Malibu Cove Beach. The sun streaked the sky orange and red as we were to meet Jesse, Chase, and some other friends for a bonfire. Kat was about to shut the back car door when she shrieked, "Wait, wait, my hoodie. I need it."

I was already ten steps ahead of her with a lightweight folding aluminum beach chair stuck under one arm and a small cooler of beer in the other. I rolled my eyes and huffed. "Come on, Princess. Let's go." My voice betrayed my impatience. Jesse would be there. Despite endless efforts to push him out of my mind, his hard hunky body, with his unruly locks of hair falling in his eyes, kept invading my reverie. *What the heck was wrong with me?*

Jason had called earlier in the morning. Luckily, I was on the elliptical machine at the gym so I had a good excuse to hit the ignore button. It wasn't until later that I returned his call. I chastised myself for not missing him while he was away for his grandma's birthday, and my guilt made me nervous about going to the bonfire. Jason would be back in town tonight and although I felt obligated to see him, I had put him off with some lame excuse that I needed to study. Oh, this was not good. I had managed to keep myself in line for years, be a good girl and behave. Now, some hot motocross rider had come along, with "bad boy" written all over him, and I gravitated to him like the mythological Ulysses drawn to the Siren's song.

"Okay, I'm cool now," Kat said breathlessly as she caught up to me, hoisting her guitar case, tote bag, and chair. Stepping off the asphalt parking lot, my feet sunk into the soft sand. It felt good, familiar and filled with promises of warm summer nights at the beach, cuddled close to someone who made your heart flutter, stealing a kiss while draped in the cover of darkness.

We trudged through the deep sand to the attendant and paid our fee for parking and entrance to the private beach area.

"Do you see Jenna or Tanner anywhere?"

"Not yet," Kat said, "But they're already here. Jenna texted me they came earlier, around four o'clock, to get one of the fire pits before they're all taken."

We scuffed our way past couples on blankets, with iced buckets of beer purchased from the Beach Café. An outdoor patio area, attached to the restaurant, opened to the stretch of sand that belonged to the private beach. Food and beverages could be purchased at the Beach Café, but we brought our own since the prices of alcoholic drinks were a little steep there.

"There they are." I dropped the small plastic cooler to the ground and waved.

"Where? I can't carry all of this stuff much longer," she whined.

"Right over there to our right. Follow me."

Kat struggled with all of the items slung onto her petite frame. We dragged our feet in the sand as we made our way to the group including Jenna and Tanner, and released our chairs, with a clatter, in a pile on the sand. Kat heaved a loud sigh of relief.

"You're such a wimp, Kat," I laughed. "I wasn't meant to be a pack animal, you know. I have to be careful of my hands. I don't want to ruin them and not be able to play guitar. That's my living now."

"Hey, Kat. Hey, Niki." Jenna said as she approached, holding an amber beer bottle in one hand. "Good to see you two hot chicks." She gave us each a hug. "What's not good for your hands?"

"Strenuous weight lifting," Kat said, like we were all idiots for not knowing.

"Come on and set up your chairs by the fire." Jenna laughed. We had been friends for years and she knew how much of a drama queen Kat could be.

I scanned the figures seated around the fire pit, searching unobtrusively for Jesse's familiar outline. I unfolded my chair and dug the legs into the sand. Damn, I didn't see him anywhere. I had hoped he would come. Maybe he got sidetracked, or held up at work. God, it was like high school all over again, all giddy, hoping to see the hot guy in the halls.

"Kat, do you remember back when I first met you, sophomore year in high school?"

Kat plopped down in her chair next to mine. She opened her guitar case and carefully removed an acoustic guitar, sanded and waxed to a honey-yellow finish. Her slender fingers pulled at the strings, as we talked. "Yeah, Niki, how could I forget? You had just come back to California after boarding school. You were so different then." She glanced back and forth between the guitar head and her fingers, as she tuned the strings.

"I know. I was a mess back then." I pulled a bottle of Corona from my little blue cooler and popped off the top. "Do you think people can change? I mean change for good. Or will they just go back to their old self someday, given enough time?" I took a long draw on my beer.

"Mmm, maybe. It's hard to say. Why?" She paused in her tuning and looked straight at me with a changed demeanor. "What's wrong, hon? What's bothering you?"

When needed, Kat could be serious and drop the dumb blonde act, and each time she did, it reminded me why we were such good friends.

"Spill it," she said.

"Jason called earlier. He's on his way back."

"Oh my God, is this about Jason? You need to let that one go. He is such a drag. There's more than one fish in the sea and what you need is lobster, baby, the best and tastiest, not some gray flatfish." She giggled and stopped talking long enough to take the beer I opened for her. She noticed that I wasn't laughing. "Hey, I don't really mean what I say about Jason...well, okay, maybe I do, but it's just that I want the best for you, Niki. You deserve it."

"But he's the kind of guy every girl wants—steady, good job, prospective future. And my dad loves him. The kind of guy I *should* want." I stared into the fire. "Something inside of me just keeps resisting."

"You're resisting for a good reason. Besides, you haven't dated him for very long. Just tell your dad, you are old enough to pick your own boyfriend." She turned her focus back to her strings.

"Oh God, he's already pissed at me for moving out. Now this will send his blood pressure sky-high. Plus he doesn't know about my doubts regarding law school. He doesn't even know I've started classes at the Fashion Institute."

"Oh, shit. Niki, you're turning into quite a rebel. I love this new side of you." Her eyes laughed.

"Yeah, he's going to have a fit when he finds out. He might cut me off altogether. Don't be surprised if you see me down in Hollywood, standing on the street with a cardboard sign next to the homeless people. I'm not cut out for that shit." I was trying to make light of the situation for the moment, knowing my dad's hot temper and controlling attitude.

What scared me more than my dad was this desire that was rumbling in the depths of my being—rumblings that were awakened the moment I met someone who was a lot like the old me, the uncontrolled, unsanctioned me. I thought I had put away the old rebellions for good, years ago when I came back from boarding school. Now that Pandora's Box had been opened, I was terrified that, once let out, part of me would never be contained again.

"Do you think your dad would really do that? Cut you off financially?"

I just shrugged and took another drink of my beer.

"I doubt it. He still feels guilty for all that happened back when Mom died. But what if my dad was right after all? What if the best thing for me is to eventually marry a safe, boring guy?" I looked down and picked at the damp label on my beer bottle, teasing off shreds and flicking them into the fire.

"What are you talking about, Niki? You don't want a dull life with a lame-ass husband."

I slouched back in my chair, exasperated. "No. On the one hand, I feel liberated finally doing what I want, and on the other hand, I feel guilty and nervous going against Dad, who is the voice of reason. What am I gonna do, Kat? What am I supposed to do?"

Jesse was part of the mix, hell, he was the catalyst for all of my inner turmoil, but I stopped short of revealing that to Kat. I could feel the tension rising from the depths of my stomach. Just talking about it, giving a voice to my feelings, made them seem larger than life. It was nervewracking, and I knew that my excitement about seeing Jesse added acid to the toxic stew already brewing inside.

Kat stopped strumming the strings on the guitar and reached over to put her arm around me. "Hey, hey now, it's all gonna be alright. Don't worry so much about your dad, just sit down and have a heart-to-heart with him, tell him how you feel and I'm sure he'll understand. Taking risks is part of life. Part of growing up. Maybe you will fail, but you can't let your fear stop you from trying. What would your mom say if she were here now giving you advice?"

"Probably what you just said." I blew out a long breath and stared into the fire that Jenna's boyfriend had made. The wind blew and the hairs on my arms prickled and stood up.

"Hello, ladies." The low vibrato of a familiar male voice caressed my ears. My pulse quickened and I turned around.

Kat jumped up out of her chair and practically catapulted herself onto Jesse. She squeaked, "Hi, Jess," and gave him a hug, holding her guitar by the neck. Jesse swung a bottle of beer in one hand, looking delicious in the dark, with the golden glow of the bonfire reflecting on his face. Oh, that uncontrollable hair of his. It hung just right; just enough in his eyes to drive me crazy and just enough to get him to run his hand through it. I loved that push. It was a seductive movement that showed the underside of his upper arm, the tender side. As if it said, "I'm vulnerable now."

I prepared myself to stand and give the "hello" hug. Did he know how difficult it would be with wobbly legs? How much control was needed to keep it at a simple "hello" hug and not jump into his arms? This was exactly what stirred my inner fears, the powerful control he had over me. I stood up and greeted him, forcing myself to keep a lot of air between us as I hugged, although secretly, I wanted to run my tongue up his bicep, and drag it across that sexy hot tattoo.

"Are you alone?" Kat asked. "Here, come sit by me, Jesse."

I feigned acting all casual, but my heart twitched with a pang. I wanted him next to me.

"Kat is gonna play her guitar for us. She has a super voice," I said.

"Aww," Kat replied. "Niki is my biggest fan. Actually, I think you're my only fan, Niki." She looked at me, laughing.

"That's not true. I've seen you play gigs and the rooms are packed," I continued. "She's really good, like good enough for 'American Idol' or something. You should audition, Kat. Next time they are in Hollywood. I'm serious."

Jesse stood behind us, one hand shoved in the pocket of his board shorts and the other holding his beer, watching me. He hadn't taken Kat's invitation to sit next to her. I felt the heat of a blush rise to my cheeks. This was awkward. He appeared restless, then motioned to where Chase stood, talking with a circle of friends.

"Chase is over there. I'm gonna go say hi to those guys for a minute." He smiled a beautiful white smile at me, took a sip of his beer, and pierced me with his gaze again. "Be right back," he said to my eyes. He didn't break his stare until the last possible moment before he turned. A tingle corkscrewed and twisted in my stomach, all the way down to the area between my legs. This guy was going to be so much trouble for me.

"Wow," Kat went back to plucking the guitar strings. "That was really obvious."

"What?" I bit my lip and looked down at my feet.

"Hell, he nearly fucked you with his eyes just now." She let out a short breath with her words. "I mean, Jesus Christ, Niki, if you didn't see that you're blind."

I cringed inside and stared down at my beer. A mass

of blackness invaded my peripheral field of vision, closing it down like the aperture of a camera lens. I squeezed the neck of the bottle. I saw small shards of amber glass shatter in my hand, the heavy part of the bottom piece fall to the sand. I stood there staring through tunnel vision at sharp pieces lying in the palm of my shaking hand. Slowly, I picked up a pointed piece. I turned over my other forearm. The sheen of my smooth skin mesmerized me and invited the glass. I saw the point of the glass drag across its surface. It trailed a path of bright red. I thought quite possibly I might fly away. Looking down at my feet, I saw crimson teardrops spatter the sand below.

"Niki. Hey, Niki." Kat's steady voice pierced my illusion, dissolving the hallucination. My field of vision expanded, and opened again. My weight settled in the center of my body.

"Where did you go there? It seemed like you spaced out for a while," she laughed nervously. "Here, hand me your empty bottle. We don't want it to break and leave glass all over the beach. Someone might step on it and get hurt."

I watched her take the bottle out of my hand.

"Sit down, girl. You look like you just saw a ghost." She strummed a soft soothing melody on her guitar.

I glanced down at my feet and everything was right again, the sand looked like it should in the light of the fire. I sat down in my chair and took a deep breath, slowly rubbing the smooth clear skin on my forearm.

"Kat, I, I..." I didn't know what to say. My emotions split me apart. I didn't want to hurt Kat, but I was sliding down a slippery slope with Jesse. I didn't want to face Jason, who was on his way home, and I didn't want to disappoint my dad.

"It's okay, Niki." Her gaze focused on her hands, working up and down the guitar. "Don't sweat the load. I know you are crushing on Jesse. Go for him, girl. I saw the way he looked at you."

"But, but—argh, I feel like a jerk."

"Nah, sweetie. It's cool. I'm fine with it. I noticed how he eyed you at the gym earlier. It was all over for me and Jesse, right then and there."

"Don't hate me."

"Never, hon. Nothing can ever come between us, especially not some hunky guy. You're every girl's best friend. Come on, let's have a good time and enjoy this beautiful summer night on the beach." She started playing a song, and my thoughts turned to Jesse. I wanted to go to him.

I stood up and stretched my legs. "I'm gonna go mingle. Do you mind?"

Kat looked up with a soft smile, "Go find him already."

"Thank you, Kat. You're the best."

"Just give me a heads up if you end up going home with him."

I gasped. "No way. I just met him...and you know...Jason."

I weaved my way through groups of people. As I passed by the fire, Tanner had his arms wrapped around Jenna and they swayed to the soft melody of Kat's guitar. I pushed on to another group gathered near the café. The patio was lit up with multicolored lights, flanking the beams that held up a gauzy sun canopy. At first, I observed Jesse from a distance, taking a few moments to admire his stature, to read him unobtrusively. Was he really a disaster waiting to happen? I tried to take an objective point of view as my eyes traced his silhouette. He had an athletic solid frame and was tattooed on his right biceps. In him was a generally recognized quality of confidence. Nothing scared him. The way he talked so easily in front of people…he had a fearless self-assurance that set him apart.

Jesse saw me closing the gap between us, and broke away from the group to meet me. My nerves were frayed. My stomach felt like I just hit the first drop on the roller coaster. I stopped and waited for his path to meet mine. I didn't want to join the group he was talking with and have to make polite conversation. I wanted to talk to him, just him and no one else.

"Do you always come to these 'shindigs' looking devastatingly beautiful?"

I nearly dropped my beer, painfully aware that my mouth hung open. He smiled a heartstopping pearly-white smile and pushed his unruly hair out of his eyes. *Damn, he is fine.* I froze, speechless. Words wouldn't come; my mouth was as dry as the Sahara.

"Hi," I managed to crackle. Oh, that sounded really smooth. My greeting was a chicken crackle. I cleared my throat, ducked my head down and blushed in the dark. "Let's try that again. Hi, Jesse." I laughed. He did too, and I was glad to see my blunder amused him.

"Enjoying the bonfire?"

"Yeah, I love going to the beach. It's really beautiful here in the summer at night. It's one of the things I missed the most when I lived in New York." I forced myself not to stare at him. I dropped my head to my feet and kicked at the sand.

"Wait, what? You lived in New York? I'm from New York, well, upstate New York. When did you live there?"

My eyes rose to his chest, with the T-shirt he wore stretched tight across its expansiveness. They tracked the ripple of muscles shifting under the fabric as he tilted his beer bottle to catch the last few drops.

"Oh, a long time ago, before high school. I went to a boarding school there." I locked my gaze on a small mound of sand I raked to the side with my foot. When I lifted my head, he had a perplexed look on his face. He shot a glance over to the fire and back.

"Would you like to go for a walk on the beach?"

*Oh my God.* Being alone with Jesse on a warm summer night was tempting. The few butterflies stirring in my stomach now swarmed to a thousand. I wrung my hands and glanced over to where Kat played her guitar.

I let out a breath.

"I'd love to. Let's grab a beer from my cooler to take with." Agreeing to go with him came so easily to my lips. I said it so willingly, yet I had Jason to deal with. Jason, who had no clue this was happening. Jason, who would be blindsided. My stomach constricted. The guilt could've been wrung out of it like a wet sponge. "The heart wants what the heart wants," and although I felt I was on the cusp of a journey filled with both roses and thorns, I pushed that thought aside.

I scooped the last two bottles from the cooler. Kat gave me a nod and a wink, without breaking the rhythm in her song, playing and singing softly by the fire. I handed one to Jesse; he twisted off the cap and flipped it into the embers. I faced him, my eyes seeking his for direction.

"Come." He jerked his head in the direction of the open beach. I followed willingly into the darkness, my heart pounding. We pushed off in the soft sand, my feet slipping a little out of my sandals as I walked. A full moon was forming at the edge of the sky. He slowed down when he saw me shifting my weight, and tripping in the sand ruts.

"Do you wanna walk or sit?" He stretched his arm in a sweeping motion, opening to the expanse of the ocean view before us. "Isn't this fantastic?"

I caught up next to him and laughed. "Yes, I love it."

"Do you know what I see?"

"No, what?" I pulled my long dark hair around to the

side with my free hand, as the night breeze whipped it across my face.

"I see a dirt track. I could kick up about a ton of this sand riding my motorcycle up and down the beach, doing donuts in the sand. Woo…" He motioned in the air as if he gripped the handlebars and revved the throttle. His expression beamed, lost in thoughts of riding. I laughed at his pantomime of a wild ride and he exhaled with a whoosh, shaking his head.

"Wow, that's never gonna happen." He stomped his foot and looked at the sand. "Who gives a shit anyway?"

Even in the darkness I could see his sadness. The smile faded from his face. He kicked at the sand and walked, leaning his upper body in a motion for me to follow. I fell in beside him, indulging the silence in the night air. I peered into his down-turned face and asked, "Why will that never happen?" His forlorn face stabbed at my heart. Something had hurt him. Or someone? In one moment my problems were gigantic, in the next they seemed minuscule.

"I mean…you're not allowed to ride motorcycles on these beaches. You'd get a ticket. But that wouldn't stop you, would it? So supposing you could get your bike here, why can't you ride your motorcycle on the beach?"

Jesse lifted his left hand in the air and wiggled his fingers, splayed them out, then formed a fist. "This." He looked at his hand and dropped his arm to his side.

"I injured my hand...and leg...in an accident, the last race I was in. It wasn't a clean break, so I needed surgery on both my hand and leg. It's complicated."

"Oh. Isn't it healed by now? It looks fine to me."

Jesse plopped down on the sand and rested his elbows on his bent knees. I followed suite and sat cross-legged next to him. I sensed a story was about to erupt. Needles prickled my skin. I wanted to know his story and everything about him. Our walk had taken us far enough from the bonfire to be secluded from the others, enough to tempt fate.

"It's taking longer than I thought. I mean, who gets a broken leg or broken hand and it takes this long to heal? I want my hand to have the precision needed to work the clutch. That's on the left handlebar of a bike. I have a little gripping ability, but not enough, it's not tight enough." His eyes followed the waves.

"I see," I said softly. I hadn't realized the severity of it all. I felt like an insensitive fool. "And your leg?"

"The left leg is used to shift the gears. On a bike it's the foot that clicks the shift, up for first gear, then down for the others. That kind of movement takes refined muscle coordination. It's one thing if a person rides for fun, but someone like me, a racer...well, you get the picture."

Impulsively, I reached out and took his left hand, stroking it. He locked his eyes on me, brimming with frustration.

"Niki, it's not just that I can't make a living racing,

it's the thought that I may never be able to ride in a competition again that scares me the most. I need to feel the freedom of racing. Riding soothes my soul. At first, right after the accident, I was lost, didn't give a damn about anything. I wanted to exist without responsibility, without faith or friends or warmth. But now, well," he gazed into my eyes. "I have a feeling that good things are happening and everything's going to look much better in the future."

"You're crazy. I'm sure it will heal fine and you will be back competing sooner than you think." His eyes slipped over my face in the dark until they found my eyes.

"And you're crazy beautiful."

My pulse picked up speed, racing through my body. Touching Jesse's hand made me feel secure, warm and special. It started at my toes and filled me all the way up to my smile. He glanced down at my hand stroking his, then back up to my face.

"I didn't mean to...I mean, with my hands..." My head was light and dizzy. Suddenly, I was aware of my breathing, aware of his touch, aware of how fatefully close our bodies had come to each other.

"Your hands? They don't offend me. What if I *want* your hands on me?" He said in a low voice.

The visual of my hands on Jesse's bare skin made my stomach drop. It was exactly what I wanted. We sat in the darkness on the beach, locked in an intense gaze for what seemed like an eternity of silence. And yet, he didn't withdraw. My skin burned like fire, from the mere touch of his hand.

"I, I…" My words caught in my throat, I couldn't find enough air on the entire beach to breathe.

Jesse adjusted his position closer me, and took my hand in both of his. Stroking and kissing, he pressed his lips to my hand, gently rubbing the back side against his cheek. Logic dictated I should pull my hand away but my emotions battled against it.

"I really want to kiss those lips of yours," he murmured.

My lips parted, my breath came ragged. All I saw in front of my face were his perfectly kissable lips, and he so much as said he wanted me to touch him. To hell with Jason. The desire to be in Jesse's arms, to feel his touch, to kiss his lips, was an uncontrollable hurricane. I couldn't have stopped it if I tried. But he could. And he did.

I sat transfixed, leaning in for the kiss, lips next to his, the scent of shave cream lingering on his skin, when the look in his eyes shifted. He gently laid my hand in my lap, leaned back and took his hands away.

"You have a boyfriend." He cocked his head to the side and blinked at me.

The ocean rolled and the crashing sound of water invaded my senses. Dammit, this was an unpredictable quality for a "bad boy." My heart sank. I wanted him to be bad, so I wouldn't have to feel guilty for what I was about to do to Jason.

It was hard to swallow. I couldn't look him in the eye. "I don't really…I mean, we broke up." I bobbed my head up and down and pursed my lips. "Yup. We broke up. A day…a couple days ago, yeah, couple days." He stalled out for a moment. I could see the gears churning in his head. My heart pounded out of my chest. I felt like an idiot. I thought I saw a look in his eyes.

Jesse leaned in and tucked a strand of hair behind my ear. His fingers traced down my cheek and caught my chin in his hand, tilting my head back. My lips spontaneously parted for him and I felt his warm sweet breath. He pressed his lips to mine and the sandy beach fell from beneath me. My head swirled as he stroked my tongue with his, prodding and teasing. I met his advance full on, submitting to his passion, blood rushing in my veins, spiking higher and higher with each stroke of his tongue. Dragging my lower lip between his teeth, he gently pulled away. I was caught breathless.

"No boyfriend? That was just a little taste of what we could have. We'll see if you have a boyfriend by tomorrow."

I fell back reeling, intoxicated by his kiss, basking in the magnetic energy that was privately and uniquely ours. An energy that never existed on the planet until now. A new creation that burst into life, in one single igniting moment.

My back pocket buzzed.

*What the fuck?*

"Do you need to get that? You can. Go ahead." He sat back into his previous position, staring out to the horizon over the ocean. I knew who it was. I didn't want to look but it was like seeing an accident on the side of the road. I had to look.

I grabbed my phone. "It's just a text."

*I'm home. Can't wait to see you. Jason.*

The blush that rose to my cheeks was not visible in the darkness, yet I was sure Jesse saw it. He had seen the text. We sat close enough for a kiss, so we were close enough for him to see the screen in the darkness.

My face fell. I was at a loss for words. I shut down the screen as fast as possible. I rolled up onto one butt cheek and shoved the stupid thing back into my pocket.

"I suppose we should go back," I mumbled, as I scrambled to get up.

"Yeah, I suppose…" He stood up and brushed the sand off the seat of his shorts. He placed his hands on my shoulders as I turned to walk away.

"Niki. Before we go back let me just tell you, I'm not stopping until you're mine. You didn't resist the kiss just now. You didn't tell me to leave you alone, so be prepared to be stalked." He smiled, and in that smile I saw his determination.

I giggled and flushed. "We'll see." Destiny hit the download button on my life and there was no stopping it. I fixed my eyes on the light of the bonfire in the distance, as we walked the short way back. My emotions were caught between a rock and a hard place. What the hell was I going to do now? The answer loomed over me like the proverbial elephant in the room, but before I could face it, I needed a good long girl talk session with Kat.

# CHAPTER 14 - Stalking

## *Jesse*

"You told her you're going to stalk her?" Chase asked. "Are you fucking kidding me? I mean, that's really the way to get a girl." He laughed and pitched a wet bar rag, hitting me in the face.

"You dickhead. That towel is gross." I flung it to the ground. "I'm gonna have to kick your ass tonight."

"Tonight? Sorry, dude, don't have time for any ass-kicking. I have a training session at the gym."

Chase picked up a couple water bottles and tossed them up in the air like a juggler.

"What the hell are you doing?"

"Practicing to be a flair bartender."

"You mean, a *gay* bartender. What are you gonna do? Join the freaking circus?"

"No, asshole, a *flair* bartender. I want to be good enough to work in Vegas as a bartender."

"No way. You're shitting me."

"I even invented my own specialty drink."

"What's it called? Chase's Pussy Drink?" I laughed. "Is it a little pink drink to attract all the girls?"

"Jackass." His face went deadpan. "It's called Chase's Chaser. It's made with layers of liquor in a martini glass. The bottom layer is red, then yellow, and blue on top. The final touch—I light it on fire right before I serve it to the ladies, and they love it. I can even breathe fire."

"I hope that gets you far in life." I yanked his chain.

"As long as it scores points with the ladies. They eat this shit up." He landed the last bottle between his head and shoulder and balanced it there.

"Just keep acting like a panty liner and *that's* what will get you far with the ladies." He threw a bottle at me. I ducked and laughed. "Hey, watch it!" It hit the wall with a bang, but luckily didn't bust open.

My uncle probably wouldn't appreciate us dickin' around like this in his bar. Kenny was the same cool guy I knew years ago, and I wanted him to know I took my job seriously. He was doing me a solid, putting me up and giving me a job at his bar. Jimmy was right, taking a break from my fucked-up life in New York was exactly what I needed. I no longer felt like a fucking waste of sperm, like the only reason I was alive was because my dad forgot to pull out. Ever since I came to California, I hadn't been drinking as much and now that I'd met Niki, life was looking like blue skies ahead.

She was beautiful, smart, and funny. She was firmly

planted in my head now and I sure as hell wanted her to stay there. I was consumed with Niki. All I had on my mind was having her in my arms, pressed against my chest, her soft lips on mine again and…Oh shit, time to adjust the family jewels. She had that effect on me. But I liked it and I schemed up ways to get to see her again. Damn, I really *was* a stalker.

"Well, if you think you're going to get Niki, you had better step up your game man, cause…you know about Jason, right?"

"She's gonna dump him. Wait and see. She'll send him packing."

"I wouldn't be so sure, dude. Jason's got you beat hands down. Sorry to say. I mean, I don't want to be the bearer of bad news, but he's already a lawyer, plus he's in with her dad." Chase handed me a cutting board and pointed to a bowl full of lemons that needed slicing. "And you? You have nothing going on right now, except your panty-dropping good looks and charisma."

"You're such an ego booster, Chase. I feel like crushing one of your testicles right now, and I say that shit with love. Way to be there for me." I raised an eyebrow and tipped my head as I picked up a lemon. He wasn't making this easy for me. All the more of an indication that Niki was something really special. If he's sticking up for her this much, she must be dynamite. I grinned from ear to ear.

Chase checked the bar clock. "You can take your lunch break first today."

"Great. I have some stuff to do anyway. I'll see you later," I said as I filled the "set-up" trays with lemon wedges. I skipped out the door of the bar and hoofed it over to Fourth Street Promenade. My cell phone buzzed in my pocket. *A text.* I pulled it out. It was Kat:

*Now is the time, lover boy.*

I pounded letters of the alphabet on the screen as I walked,

*Are you're sure today is the day?*

*Yes, yes. Jesus, you're like a lost little boy. I told you a hundred times, today is the day.*

*My bad. What if I'm too late?*

*Lame. Be there or be six feet under. :)*

The screen went dead. I shoved the phone back in my pocket and pushed my hand through my hair. I pulled up short as I rounded the first stone corner of the sandwich shop next to a cell phone store on the pedestrian mall. I exhaled and leaned up against the side of the building, tense, waiting, heart pounding. I lifted my sunglasses off my nose for a clearer view. Nothing. Just a million motherfuckers walking around this place. *Shit.* This wasn't gonna work.

I had come to catch Niki on her lunch break from her fashion design classes. Kat had tipped me off, but now I was about to chicken out. What if she didn't want to see me?

I spotted her, breathtakingly beautiful, as she walked across the mosaic brick pavement, towards the sandwich shop. My eyes zeroed in on the movement of her tits, bouncing as she walked. My eyes had a mind of their own. Her long dark hair flipped in the breeze, caught on the upstroke of her bounce. My mouth was dry. She closed the gap between us. Her head was down, with a large bag slung over one shoulder and her eyes hidden behind large sunglasses. *Damn*. Did she see me? Did she *want* to see me? I played it cool. She got closer. I stared in the other direction. She was practically on top of me. She wasn't looking. She didn't see me. She was about to walk right past me.

"Niki." My voice was a little too loud and she startled.

"Oh, Jesus!" She caught her breath. "You scared the shit out of me." She held one hand to her breast and slipped off her sunglasses.

"Excuse me, miss. Did anyone ever tell you, you look a lot like my first wife?"

She laughed and rolled her eye. I wanted to get lost in those eyes.

"First wife? You've got balls. How many do you plan to have?"

"Well, rumors have been told…"

She raised her eyebrows and smirked. "What are you doing here?" She pulled her chin in and gave me a stern look. "Are you stalking me? Wait, how did you know I would be here?"

"Just chance." Her eyes narrowed with disbelief. "Seriously, I came here to…um…" I looked up and saw the sign in front of the cell phone store. "I had to fix my cell phone. Yeah." I nodded. She turned slightly and looked at the cell phone store, then back to me.

"Oh, what's wrong with your phone?"

I still had my phone in my hand, waving it around as we talked. "It...it's broken."

She nodded, her head bobbed up and down.

"Uh huh...I see. And how is it broken?" She narrowed her eyes speculatively at me.

"It has...um, a...broken screen. Yeah, broken screen." She craned her neck to peer at the phone in my hand. I flipped it over so she couldn't see the screen.

"It doesn't look like it has a broken screen." She wrinkled her brow. "Let me see. Where?" She reached out to touch my phone. I flipped it again, screen side up, and held it out in the palm of my hand.

"Right there." I pointed to the smooth screen. "There's a crack right there." She leaned over for a closer look, nose to the screen.

"You're crazy. I don't see any crack in the screen." She straightened up.

I held the phone, screen side out, and smashed it against the stone side of the building, then laid out my palm with it. Her mouth dropped open and her eyes got wide as saucers. "See? There's the crack."

"Oh my God! Jesse, you *are* fucking crazy. You just broke your phone." Her voice squeaked and she laughed at the same time.

"I told you it was broken." I grinned.

"I can't freaking believe you just did that."

"I would break my phone any day just to have a reason to see you. Now come on, how about I take you to lunch, please? Don't say no. You'll break my heart if you say no and I don't think there's a store to fix that." I gave her my best puppy-dog eyes. She huffed and stomped her foot.

"Jesse. You are so, so…aaargh," she groaned. She was balking. My heart sank.

"I'm meeting a friend here for lunch." She waved a hand in the direction of the sandwich shop. "And I would if…you know…if I wasn't in a relationship."

"I know, I know, Jason." *Fucking Jason.* She's gotta realize it's me she wants and not Jason. I know how she kissed me. It was like warm honey covered my entire body, and she felt it too. I was in deep and there was nothing that could save me now. I wanted this woman bad. If she left, I'd be in a world of pain.

I knew I would never be her dad's favorite. I'd be thinking the same thing if I were in his shoes. But I'd changed. They don't know. They don't get how I have felt since I met my Niki. She can't just leave now.

Niki gave me the most beautiful look with her eyes. I felt like the sky was falling. I stepped in a little closer to her and reached for her arm. The urge to pull her to my chest rumbled from deep inside me. A light breeze picked up the essence of her perfume and wafted it up my nose. Her scent was heavenly.

"Please, Niki. I want to see you. Let me take you out tonight, then." I said, standing as close to her as she would let me. "Jason doesn't deserve you. I'll treat you better. Does he buy you flowers?" I leaned in closer and whispered in her ear. "When he's done, does he take his time to admire you?"

She faltered, pulled away and looked startled.

"I'm sorry, I gotta go." She turned and waved at someone. "Here comes Courtney now."

"I'm not giving up," I said. I wasn't a quitter. I didn't win all those races by giving up, but winning races was easy compared to winning Niki's heart.

She smiled and took a step backwards, ready to walk away. She gave a little laugh, shook her head and said, "You're too dangerous for me, Jesse Morrison."

"Dangerous? No, maybe a little on the wild side."

"Okay, then," she said, and started walking.

"And a stalker. I'm good at being a stalker too. I take my job seriously, so brace yourself, sweetie. You're gonna be seeing me around a lot more than you ever imagined. Don't be surprised if I rock your dream world." I raised my eyebrows with a wiggle. She gave me a wave and walked off to meet up with her friend. I spun around to head back to work. *Shit*. I needed to go to the cell phone store.

# CHAPTER 15 – Daddy's Golden Boy

## *Niki*

"You look nice, babe." Jason closed my apartment door behind him as he stepped into the living room. It had been almost two weeks since that Sunday night when he returned from his grandmother's birthday, the night I was on the beach with Jesse

"Come in, Jason. I have to get my purse and I'll be ready."

"I hope you're hungry. I've picked out a good place for us to eat."

I wrung my hands under the little white sweater I had draped over my arm. "Sure, Jason. Just give me a moment."

Jason stood stiffly in khaki pants and a white polo shirt near the entryway. He found it difficult to sit; waiting was not his forte. He preferred to pace and reorganize my knickknacks on the bookshelves, or straighten the already level pictures hanging on the walls. Just like my dad. A neat freak.

"They serve organic and vegan."

"I'm not really into vegan. Don't they have beef?" I said as I headed down the short hall to my bedroom to locate my little peach-colored purse. I don't know why he chose to forget. We'd had this conversation before. I popped back into the living room and he was on a rant.

"Ugh. You never eat beef. How can you even say that, Niki? Don't you realize how bad beef is for you? Didn't we read *The China Study* by Colin Campbell together?" He reached for the doorknob and allowed me to exit first.

"Well, yeah, but..."

"Maybe you need to read it again." The acid in my stomach rose up in my esophagus. I stared at the ground as he pulled the door shut behind us. We walked to the car and I opened my mouth to say what a lovely evening it was, but he continued.

"Campbell's findings about the link between dietary habits and health have been published in the most reputable scientific journals and now in this book. Campbell is a research scientist and his scientific studies have demonstrated that a good diet is the most powerful weapon against disease. And eating beef, or having a steak dinner with a baked potato and all the toppings, is a big 'no-no;' why, it's just a heart attack waiting to happen. It's not good for you, Niki. You need to eat healthier. I don't want to become a widower at forty."

"Well, we are not exactly married yet." I withered a

little inside. I wanted to have an enjoyable evening out, but as usual Jason's cheerless personality cloaked the entire evening with his need to control.

We had been spending our usual three nights a week together, nights scheduled by Jason. He insisted on scheduling the time according to his calendar of events. It had been nearly a week since the bonfire and every time I was with Jason I turned red with guilt, as if I wore Jesse's kiss, like a scarlet letter, burned onto my lips. I was sure Jason could see it.

I chastised myself: it was merely a kiss. No big deal. Yet my stomach swirled with anxiety. And I didn't even know why. Sure, I saw Jesse again but that was because he stalked me at the sandwich shop. And we had casually texted back and forth a bit during the week. But it was really nothing.

I re-checked the zipper on my peach purse to make sure it was shut tightly. I didn't want to chance it, that my cell phone might fall out and Jason might accidentally see the messages. Though I didn't exactly know how that could happen. *Damn it.* Jason had me all on edge, feeling too much shame, judgment, and mistrust.

All week I asked myself, why had I let Jesse into my life? In every private moment I had to myself, thoughts of him would invade my mind, like the chirping of crickets on a warm summer night. And I caught myself lost in a daydream of being in Jesse's arms instead of Jason's. It happened, all by itself, without thinking.

What is it that Jesse and I have to experience together? Why have we been brought into each other's lives? Who is moving the strings and for what reason? Will I be able to understand all this—ever?

The waiter sat us at our table. The restaurant had modern, sleek wooden and chrome decor. Very bland, like the food—like Jason.

"I really wish you would have gone with me to the birthday. Everyone was asking about you and why you weren't there." He rearranged the water glass and silverware on the table in front of him to his satisfaction.

"I'm sorry, Jason, I never met your grandmother and I felt it was too soon in our relationship for that kind of thing. That's why I decided not to go with you. And besides, I had an assignment to finish."

Jason frowned, placed his elbows on the table, and laced his fingers together under his chin. "I can't believe you're wasting your time with this designer thing. You seem to be making a lot of bad choices lately. It's such an illogical idea to take classes in fashion design. I mean seriously, aren't you going to be a lawyer like me and your father? Are you going to waste your life designing clothes for no-brain teenagers? You were at the top of your class, Niki. You're about to waste your four-year degree. You need to think about the future and which one is the most logical and profitable career choice."

"You sound like my fucking father." Jason's face

paled in surprise of my choice of words. "You don't understand. I need to do this because it's *my* choice. All my life I've done what my dad wants. My entire life's been a fraud, afraid to be myself, like being me somehow wasn't enough. I walked around on pins and needles, living in that house with him, convinced that I wasn't good enough, smart enough, lovable enough…ha, I even believed that in order to be happy and please him, I had to become better, smarter, and even more lovable. I walked around like a fucking robot, tucked my real feelings away. I wasn't allowed to be sad when Mom died. Good girls aren't sad. And I got angry when Dad sent me away to boarding school because he couldn't deal with me and my emotions. But good girls aren't supposed to be angry. Good girls don't act that way, right? They just get called 'bitch' for showing their emotions. I hid from my feelings too long, Jason. I hid a very important part of me. My creative part, and I'm scared to death that if I don't start living my life the way I want, it'll be harder and harder to hear myself, my authentic self…and a part of me will be lost forever."

I gulped and tried to calm myself. There wasn't enough air in the room, the heat gathered inside of it was like a sudden, awful hand over my mouth. I hurried to sip my water, before I had a meltdown. I took a deep breath. "I like designing. When I woke up this morning I had an idea in my head, and at the end of the day, there was a design on the table. My creation, a piece of me, now existed, and didn't earlier. Can you do *that* as a lawyer?"

He sat like stone, not breathing a word while I poured my emotions out all over the table. He calmly took his hands down to his lap and cleared his throat.

"Niki, that kind of career isn't a profession, like lawyer. It won't make you any money. In order to have a profitable career in fashion design, you would have to make it really big as a designer. And what are the chances of that? Who says you're really good at it? The fashion school you are attending tells all the applicants how talented they are. This school is in the business of making money. It's a *career school*, Niki, not a university. They'll gladly take the money of every starry-eyed girl who is willing to pay the tuition. At the most, you might make a decent living for a few years but then, as with any artistic endeavor, another young fresh artist/designer will come along and 'bam'—you're out of business. Honestly, Niki, you're wasting your time with this silly idea of yours."

"You arrogant asshole. You have no idea, Jason. Did you even listen to me? You don't even know me. And what the hell do you know about fashion design anyway? It's my passion. Don't judge me. You don't know shit."

"Whoa, whoa, easy now, tiger. I didn't mean it that way. You're probably great at 'fashion design' and really, it's not that important to be creative. Look. Here's what you can do, Niki. Be a lawyer, have a good income and career, and you can do something with your design stuff in your spare time…as a hobby. That's it. There you go. That's what you will do. That is what you *need* to do. It'll make your father proud."

If I had something to throw at him I would have. Jason hadn't heard a word I'd said. How dare he criticize my life choices? I was about to explode in his face, but thankfully, the waiter came to our table.

"Ah, the food has arrived. Let's eat," Jason said with a smug face.

A young waiter with a long low ponytail, wearing very "I love Earth Day" attire, placed a plate of a vegan entree in front of me. Between the lackluster food and Jason's attack on my ability to run my own life, I wished I had a big, fat juicy steak to cut into, with blood oozing onto the plate from the first cut.

I picked up my fork and held it in my fist with the force of a death grip. I stared at the food, not sure I could eat right now. My blood boiled. I was more than pissed.

"What's wrong? You look mad," he said evenly and cut into his food.

I shoved a forkful of the pasty-white shit into my mouth and chewed viciously. I swallowed hard before it was completely chewed.

"What's wrong?" My indignation rose to suicidal heights. "You don't even see it, do you? You don't see what a selfish controlling prick you are."

Jason lowered his knife and fork and leaned forward.

"Maybe we should talk about this later."

I dropped my fork on the table. I was done with him and his control issues.

"No, we are going to fucking talk about it right now. Who are you to tell me what to do? Seriously. You're not my dad. I know what I want and I know I have the talent. It's all clear to me now, you don't support my dreams. How do you think that will work in a fucking relationship?"

"I really wish you would calm down and stop swearing like a sailor—" He started to speak, but I was on a roll and I plowed ahead.

"Do you suffocate everything that comes your way? You can't put me in a box, Jason, like you always do in your super-organized, super-clean world, so things won't get messy. I'm sorry Jason, that's just not me. Maybe I want to be messy, maybe sometimes I am unorganized. Just let me be myself."

"Niki, Niki. Life is not always about doing what you want. Grownups must take responsibility for their actions. You can't do whatever you please."

Oh great, now he was placating me. I rolled my eyes and sat back in my chair.

"Niki, I don't know what's gotten into you lately. And on another issue, what were you thinking, moving in with Kat? She's the most irresponsible person. You know what, you should move in with me. I have more to offer you than a cheap apartment with a crazy out-of-control boy toy. I have a good job and…"

I pushed my plate away.

"I'm done here. I can't eat this." I wiped my mouth with the napkin. "I see it now, Jason. You're always going to argue, get things going the way you plan. You are a lawyer and you will argue until you die. I'll never win. You will always put yourself first. Well, damn it, I refuse to live that way."

"Niki, what do you mean?"

"Jason, I used to think we could make it as a couple, but now I know that we're not meant for each other." I looked up to the ceiling, as if the answer had been hanging over me all along. "I refused to see it before, but it's so clear. You are my dad, exactly like my dad, and the last thing in the world I want is to marry my dad."

"Hold on. Now you're just being silly. I don't know why you would compare me to your father. I'm nothing like him." He finished his meal and leaned in again. "You've had a long week and so have I. You're tired and I have an early meeting. Let me drive you home. Once you've calmed down, I'm sure you will think differently in the morning. Sleep on it and we will talk about you moving in with me tomorrow."

Oh my God. This guy was a brick wall. I folded my arms across my chest.

"There's nothing to talk about. I'm done with this. There's a girl for you who is just your type, but I'm not that girl. I want the opposite of you. I want to experience life, and live it. I don't care about status, or money. I care about joy, passion, dreams, and fulfillment." I flung my hands up in the air. Jason stared at me blankly. For once he was speechless.

"We are done. Let's just move past this."

Jason paid the bill and we left the restaurant in silence. I politely thanked him for opening my car door, but the ride home was like ice water. As we pulled up in front of the apartment, I couldn't get out of the car fast enough. He parked and made a motion as if he would walk me to the door, but I was already out of the car. I didn't want him to think there would be the possibility that he was invited in.

"Stop, Jason," I said. "Don't bother. I don't want you to come in."

"Niki, please..." His eyes begged. He actually looked sad, as if his perfectly controlled exterior was on the verge of shattering. I almost felt a pang of sympathy in my heart, but if I allowed it to surface, it would just lead to the unraveling of my confidence.

I was tired of being the victim, feeling like a martyr, rather than taking responsibility for my part of all this. Being the victim felt safer because that position, that role in the relationship—hell, in my whole life—had made me feel small, and the smaller I felt, the less likely I was to be hurt again. That's why I had a very dull relationship with Jason. That was me until a week ago, the day when Jesse walked into my life, oozing of danger and excitement, and it hit me like a ton of bricks. I could only be the victim for so long before doing something about it.

I opened the door to the building and didn't look back. In my imagination, Jason stood by the car with a tear rolling down his cheek and any minute would run after me yelling, "Come back, Niki. Please, I love you." He didn't, though.

I stepped a foot onto the stairs to my apartment, as I heard the engine start up and he drove away. So predictable. I could have looked back to watch his car leave the parking lot, but it wouldn't have revealed any new information and I didn't want him to have the satisfaction of seeing me look back. Looking back is a sign of regret.

"Niki, what's wrong?" Kat was perched on a small stool with her guitar in front of a microphone mounted on a stand. This was how she practiced for gigs. She used a small amplifier to hear the quality of her voice as it sounded while performing.

"I just broke up with Jason." I sniffed. Tears formed the corner of my eyes. I was disappointed with myself for crying about it. I wanted to be stronger than that.

"Shut the fuck up. No way." She stopped playing the guitar. She was probably happy to hear this news. She didn't think Jason was the right one for me anyway. I kicked off my shoes and flopped on the couch like a wet noodle.

"I should feel liberated and powerful. Hell, I just took back my life. Instead I feel like I hurt him, and I really didn't want to do that." I looked down at my summer dress and picked at imaginary lint.

Kat laid her guitar on the floor next to the stool and sat next to me on the couch. "Come here, hon. Give me a hug. Everything is going to be okay. You didn't hurt him. He's a big boy and honestly, if he didn't see this coming then he's just an idiot." She hugged and patted me. I expected her to lay into him for being a jerk and run him into the ground, but she didn't. And I was glad.

"Thanks, Kat. You're the best friend ever."

"No problem. That's what I'm here for. Now, no more tears. Okay? No guy is worth your tears. What can I do to cheer you up? Do you want to go out for ice cream?"

I laughed and wiped the tears from my face with the back of my hand. "No, Kat. I'm not five years old, but thanks. I think I'll go to my room, get into my pajama shorts and read magazines. It's been a nervewracking evening."

"Sure, hon. Just let me know if you change your mind. I'm always here."

I forced a weak smile and scooped up my purse and shoes. As soon as I shut my bedroom door I dropped the shoes and flung the purse on the bed. I tore the sun dress off over my head and fell onto the bed, feeling emotionally drained. Why were tears still pooling in my eyes? I stood up to Jason. I didn't want to cry over the breakup. I wanted to be strong. I shut the light out and rolled onto my side, lying on top of the covers in my underwear, waiting for my emotions to settle.

I stared into the darkness, letting my eyes fall on the shadows of the room, lightly illuminated from the apartment parking lot through the window. I looked up at the fan mounted in the ceiling. I wondered how much weight it could hold. The weight of a human body? Or would that much weight pull it out of the ceiling? My dark thoughts were distracted by a muffled buzz, signaling me from within my purse on the bed where I had thrown it. Jason probably wanted to get the last word in our conversation. I pulled out the phone, prepared to ignore it once I confirmed it was him.

*Hey, beautiful. Any chance you will talk to me?* It was a text from Jesse. I sat up in bed and clicked on the night light next to me.

*Do you always call your friends beautiful in text messages?*

*Only the really beautiful friends. :)*

*You're a flirt. A dangerous flirt.*

*I'm sitting here all alone on a Friday night just thinking about you.*

*You're a tease. I find that hard to believe. :)*

*Hard to believe that I am thinking about you?*

*No, hard to believe you are all alone on a Friday night. Your charming smile not working lately?*

*Just waiting for a miracle. YOU.*

*Well, miracles do happen.*

*What? There's something you're not telling me. Are you holding out on me? Are you texting me while you're with Jason? If you are—that's hot! Live dangerously and sext me something.*

*Ha. Ha! No way. Perv.*

*C'mon. Text me something dirty while he is sitting across from you.*

*In your dreams. I'm not out with him.*

*Then where is the douche-bag?*

*I don't know. I'm home by myself. Getting ready for bed.*

*Sounds nice. I could come over and tuck you in?*

*Goodnight, Jesse.*

*Hey! I thought tonight was a Jason night?*

I couldn't believe it. Jesse had been stalking me for so long he now knew my date nights.

*It got cancelled.*

*Are you okay?*

*I'm fine. We're taking a break.*

*What does that mean exactly? A couple of weeks apart, and then you see where you stand or what???*

*Maybe. Who knows?*

*As long as you're okay, Niki...So since you are "on a break," how about that sext? :-)*

*Back to that, are we? :)*

I grinned from ear to ear. His messages put a smile back on my face at the end of a sour night. The texts had been flying back and forth, rapidfire speed, when there was a pause. My heart jumped. He wasn't responding. Finally, another text came.

*Niki, believe in yourself. You're beautiful, very beautiful, and smart, the smartest person I know. I'm not just texting a bunch of bullshit. Seriously, I think there is something very special about you.*

*...*

*Can I take you out tomorrow night if you are free?...if you would rather wait, then soon...*

My heart melted and I sat up straighter on the bed. Fuck it, I needed this right now. I was going for it. I took a deep breath and answered.

*Took you long enough to ask. Lol. But the odds are against us.*

*Fuck the odds. We'll make our own odds.*

# CHAPTER 16 – The Showcase

## *Jesse*

Thirty more minutes and I was outta here. I rushed through my end of shift duties at work. Chase walked from the front to where I stacked boxes of vodka in the back hallway.

"So who's your prom date for tonight, Cinderella?" He was busting my chops. He knew I was in a hurry to get to a date. He tossed me a bottle of disinfectant spray and a rag.

"Niki."

Chase raised his eyebrows. "Niki?"

"Kat is performing tonight at Hotel Café in Hollywood. It's open mic night and Niki and I are going."

"No fucking way. What about..." I held up a hand. I wasn't the *National Enquirer* and didn't want to go into details right now. I told it like it was, short and sweet.

"She dumped the motherfucker."

"Huh." He snorted in disbelief.

"Technically, she says they're on a break. But I know what that means."

"What the hell, it works for me. Way to go, champ." He gave me a high five and disappeared into Kenny's office.

Ever since I came to California I had experienced "good days" and occasionally they accumulated into weeks. More and more I felt like my old self, the affectionate and charming guy my friends back in New York had cherished. And now, this girl, this incredibly amazing creature walked into my life and I felt so passionate about her. Things were finally heading in the right direction.

Tonight, after "stalking" Niki for a couple of weeks, I was going to have a real date, quality time alone with her, just the two of us. I couldn't stop thinking about her lips and kissing her again. It had been two weeks since we kissed at the beach. *Pace yourself, Jesse.* I should go slow. Very slow. I didn't want to fuck this one up, but sometimes my cock had a mind of its own. Jesus fuck, I was nauseous.

My shift was over and I hightailed it home for a quick shower before picking up Niki. I walked on air. My head was in the sky. Every fucking love song I knew ran through my mind. All of them made fucking sense now.

An hour later, I parked my truck at her apartment and skipped up the step to her door. She opened the door and *Holy shit,* she took my breath away. Her long dark hair hanging in big curls made me want to grab a fistful and pull her lips to mine. Those perfectly sculpted luscious lips. I wanted them all to myself, all over my body. She wore a light-colored, tight-fitting short dress. My eyes trailed down the length of her bare legs. They ended in those hot heels girls call "fuck me" shoes. For the love of God, dressed like that, she made it hard for me not to be a dickhead and jump her bones, right here and now.

"Damn, you look stunning, Niki."

"Thank you. I'm ready to go if you are." Her smile melted me.

I stepped back, allowing Niki to go first. The light scent of her perfume rolled across my senses as she passed. The desire to hold her hot body pressed up against mine, on cool white sheets, flashed through my mind. I put my fist to my mouth and faked a cough, to cover the involuntary groan that threatened to erupt from my throat. She thought I sneezed and sweetly said "bless you" as she stepped down to the sidewalk. She was so fucking cute and ladylike. I didn't want to jeopardize this relationship by going all "caveman" on her. I pictured myself messing up all that dark hair, as we twisted in deep kisses. It drove me crazy. She was the best thing in my sorry-ass life right now. I don't know what I did to bring on this kind of sweet karma, but I sure as hell didn't want it to go away. Fucking ever.

We rolled into the parking lot behind the Hotel Café

with just a few minutes to spare before Kat would go on stage. On the drive over, I chanted a mantra, "keep your dick in your pants, keep your dick in your pants," to myself. If I kept repeating it enough times, it might distract my urge to rip that tight dress off her body and possess her right here in the front seat of my truck. I ached for her so bad.

Open mic night was under way when we walked in. The seating area with tables and chairs was dark. The stage was bathed in bright white lights for the performers, where Kat was about to go on. A brother duo act harmonized to their last song on acoustical guitars. No tables were available up front, but that was cool. I preferred a little privacy. We scored a cozy, round booth in the back, suited to my liking, very secluded.

"This is really nice, Jesse." She sat down and I shimmied up next to her. Goose bumps rose up on my inked skin, when a strand of her long hair tickled my arm. In all my exuberance I had moved a little too close. She giggled and pulled all of her hair to one side of her neck with her hand.

*Oh fuck.*

Now my eyes were glued to her long, perfectly exposed neck. Right next to me. Within striking distance. I could just die in her arms tonight, like a fucking eighties song.

"Can I get you a drink?" I turned away, looking for the waitress. Something twitched in my pants. *Damn.*

"After last night, I need one. Relationships are not easy, even when you know in your heart it's over. Do you know what I mean?"

"It's his loss. He's an idiot for letting you go. But I'm glad he did. Finally, I get to take you out."

I searched for a waitress, but none were in sight. I stepped up to the bar and returned with a Coors Light and a glass of white wine. I leaned in with my elbows on the table, angling my body to keep her pinned under my gaze. "You know, tonight is a new beginning and I want to know everything about you." I took a swig from my beer. "Tell me, what's up with that designer school? Chase told me that you were planning on going to law school?"

Niki was in the middle of taking a sip of wine. My words interrupted her ability to swallow and she nearly choked.

"You okay? Is law school a bad word?"

"Law school, well." She gave an audible sigh. "That's a long story and it reminds me of some of the shit I've been going through lately."

"What do you mean?

"Let's just say, my dad and I don't see eye to eye on a lot of things. He wants me to go to law school and, as you know, I'm taking fashion design classes right now.
"

"Yeah, I kind of wondered about that. The day I 'stalked' you at lunch I kind of thought it was strange that you were taking fashion classes when you just got

155

your B.A."

"God, Jesse, you don't know the half of it…what it's been like for me. All these years I've done what my dad wants. And he's so intimidating and controlling."

"You're an adult; it's your life, Niki. Follow your heart. The past is history and tomorrow, well, who knows what tomorrow brings."

"That's very poetic," She chuckled. "But you don't know my dad. He's a bulldog and a fighter. He doesn't give up easily when it comes to getting his way."

"Hmm. So I take it you haven't told him yet that you're taking these fashion classes." She shook her head and pressed her lips together hard, like it was difficult for her to say what she wanted.

"What about your mom? What does she think of all this?"

"My mother died when I was twelve."

"Oh, I'm sorry."

"It's okay. It was a long time ago. My dad wasn't so, so…intense back then. We were one big happy family. I mean, he worked a lot, he's a lawyer, so what do you expect? Then everything changed."

"I know what you mean."

"After my mom died, I couldn't cope. I was too much for my dad to handle. He tried to deal with it, but he wasn't the kind of person cut out for a preteen with problems. And I was a handful, believe me. I went on rages and screamed and freaked out, I let all my emotions out, like I had no control of them. I thought that if I screamed enough, maybe I could scream away all the hurt and anger." She took a sip of wine. "Guess that strategy didn't work. My dad sent me away to boarding school in New York. Can you believe that?"

After a moment, Niki relaxed and she slumped down into her seat again. "I felt emotionally abandoned." Her gaze drifted off to a corner in the room, as if it were some imaginary day in her past. I reached out and took her hand. She gave me a little smile and I rubbed the back of her hand with my thumb. Niki was so fucking sweet; I couldn't picture anyone abandoning her. I wanted to find her dad and punch his fucking lights out. What a shithead, abandoning his twelve-year-old daughter like that.

"Didn't he even try to help you? Get you some therapy?"

"Oh, he did. The school he sent me to was not the typical kind of boarding school for rich kids. This school had therapy as their focus for troubled kids. It was supposed to be a brief stint while he figured out his next move. But it ended up being nearly four years I lived away from home, and he was no closer to understanding me then than he is now. My worst fear is, it might be too late for us to have a decent relationship, like other fathers and daughters. I have a lot of 'issues' and self-doubt as a result of it all. Thanks a lot, Dad, what an inheritance."

"You, a troubled teen? I can't see that." I said in disbelief. I couldn't picture this sweet girl ever getting in trouble.

"It's true. I'm not proud of some of the things I've done in the past, but I'm more hopeful now. I finished college, did it his way for four years. Now it's my turn to finally take control of my own life." She sat up and squared her shoulders with an air of confidence.

"That's what I like about you, Niki. I can see the determination in your eyes, there's a fire burning in there." She blushed and dropped her chin to her chest. I took her hand in both of mine and pressed it to my lips. "And like I said in my text, you are a very special person." I took a moment to drink her all in, enjoyed the tactile pleasure of her skin on my lips. It tasted good and I wanted like hell to taste the rest of her.

"You know, Niki, if you want to talk about life changes, I've got a hell of a story for you." She cocked her head to the side, curious to hear.

"Jesse Morrison? King of 'dangerous cool' has a sordid past? The guy with a trail of drooling women tripping over his heels? Why, I could throw a damn rock and hit a hundred other women, eagerly waiting for you to grace them with your presence." She was being sarcastic. I got it. I'm a dickhead.

"Don't be so hard on me. I'm a sensitive motherfucker. I watch chick flicks with a box of Kleenex, tacos, and a beer. And that tear rolling down my face at the end of the movie is not from the strong onions in my taco." She swatted my arm. It was good to see her smile. I was overwhelmed with the urge to protect her. Hell, I was a shark and although we hadn't known each other long, I already knew I would slay dragons for her.

"So, what's your story, Jesse? You came out of nowhere with your bulging biceps, a charming smile and that hot 'Carpe Diem' tattoo. I bet if I looked at your cell phone it would be blown up with messages from some poor brokenhearted girl you left in New York."

I was lost in giving little kisses to Niki's hand while she talked. I didn't want to let it go. I loved her skin on my lips. She wanted to talk, communicate, verbalize. Shit, I wanted to touch, get busy, and fuck. Reluctantly, I released her hand from my lips and set it back on the table.

"My life story is one sorry-ass story." I leaned back, ready to spill my guts. "No, I didn't leave a girl pregnant back in New York." Her eyes popped out and she sat up with her mouth open.

"I didn't say pregnant. Wait. No. Did you?" She gasped.

"No-oh. You were thinking it, though. Thanks a lot, Niki." My eyes narrowed with humor. I enjoyed watching her twist in her seat. I continued the ruse. "Now I know what you *really* think of me."

"I didn't, I didn't mean…" Her cheeks pinked up so cute when she was flustered. It was too dark in the bar to see it, but I'm sure they were bright.

"I'm kidding, I'm kidding already." She relaxed

159

again and shot me a look that threatened playful revenge. "The truth is, I'm a jackass. I was living with my brother Jimmy and his wife. I kept fucking up. I had everything going for me, my career was on fire. I was racing and doing great and then…"

"You had the accident that messed up your leg and hand, right?"

"Yeah, I did, but that's not what really fucked up my head. My mom, she's not well…she tried to commit suicide a year ago. I whine and cry that my hand will never heal, but shit, that's not what sent me into a funk, it was my mother. I felt responsible for it, you know, like if I had been there for her, instead of all over the world racing, she wouldn't have done it. If I'd been there, she wouldn't be confined to a fucking mental institution. Then the accident happened, I started drinking, drugging and, well…whoring. You know the typical guy way to deal with emotions. Push them all down and drink them away."

"Did you get help? Go for any therapy?"

"Absolutely. My therapist's name was Jack. Jack Daniels. You may have heard of him."

"Yeah, right." She pursed her lips, tucked in her chin, and looked at me with a little scold in her eyes. "Even now you are trying to dodge the issue. Hospital? Sounds serious."

"Well, it's more like a long-term care facility. She has to stay until she's well enough to be on her own." ,

Niki laid her dainty hand on my forearm. "I'm so

sorry, Jesse but don't blame yourself. These things are complicated. The human mind is mysterious and we're all driven by our emotions to do crazy stuff sometimes. I believe things happen for a reason. You're here in California, sitting with me, right now because of all that."

Niki stared into my eyes long and hard. Hers were half closed, very sexy. It would've taken an act of God to pull my gaze from her face. I moved closer. My pulse picked up, my head dizzy, and it wasn't the alcohol this time. I was careful tonight not to drink too much around Niki.

*But damn, I had to have those lips now.*

I leaned over, inhaling her scent, and slipped my hand around the nape of her neck. I pulled her to me and filled my mouth with her softness. She leaned into the kiss. *Yesss.* She submitted to my advance, twisting into the kiss, her taste on my lips when she pulled away. God, she was sexy. And sweet. Her kisses tasted fucking sweet. I swear, like candy. I couldn't believe she'd give a jerk like me the time of day, yet here she was, cuddled up next to me. I couldn't explain it. Everything was different with her, intense yet so calm. I wasn't used to this, putting myself on the line. I was raw and exposed—vulnerable, I guess, would be the word. It excited me and scared me at the same time. I found my heaven on this earth tonight.

*Fuck, look at me, I'm such a pussy.*

I was getting my groove on with Niki when Kat

announced her last song to the audience. She sounded amazing. I was surprised at her talent. I had her pegged as all looks and no brains or talent. After finishing her set, Kat came to our table and ruined my monopoly on Niki. Shit, I was already possessive of Niki's attention. I wanted her all for myself, but I was different than that other asshole she'd just dumped. I could take it slow, if she wanted. It would be hard, I mean difficult. Hard was what happened in my damn pants every time I kissed her.

After a couple of hours, we left Hotel Café with Kat and a couple of her friends who'd showed up to watch her perform. We headed to Kat and Niki's apartment for an after party. I craved more alone time with Niki, but I would be patient. Taking it slow.

## CHAPTER 17 – First Date

### *Niki*

My stomach fluttered as I waited for Jesse to pick me up. It was another summer day in California, the place where beautiful weather was included in the rent. Jesse rolled into the parking lot of my apartment complex in his big pickup truck and I hurried down the stairs to meet him.

"Ready for your tour of Santa Monica?" I asked as I crawled up into his giant truck.

"Sure, as long as you are my guide, I'll do whatever you want."

I had planned to show him the pier. It is a landmark here on the West Coast, a special place, a romantic place. Today it would be a place where I could get to know Jesse better. I was excited as we pulled into the parking lot on the wooden pier.

Older men dotted the edge of the pier with their

fishing poles, casting their lines in hopes of catching today's dinner. Kids begged their parents for yet another ride on the screaming roller coaster, while the younger ones preferred the famous merry-go-round. Scanning the beach down below, we spotted hundreds of people on bikes, roller skates, and skateboards. A small group of tourists maneuvered Segways along the narrow concrete path that stretched for miles along Santa Monica beach.

"I'll race you down to the beach," Jesse said.

He gave me a head start. I ran down the wooden stairs leading to the oceanfront as fast as I could, and soon I kicked at the sand as we strolled along the water's edge, catching our breath. Thoughts of our last walk on the beach in Malibu, the night of the bonfire, drifted into my mind. My pulse quickened in response to the memory of Jesse's kisses. Who was this guy, this hunk from New York? He had a very strong effect on me. One might call it "love at first sight." No, this was "lust at first sight." I chuckled. People don't fall in love after merely seeing each other a few weeks. Or do they? Whatever it was, it pulled me in two directions at the same time. Could I trust him? Could I trust myself? I didn't exactly have a rock-solid past when it came to emotional issues. I had a lot of hurt from my mother's death, and resentment towards my father. And then there was my step-mom, Cinnamon, practically my age.

What had I learned about good loving relationships? In my world, love had been a difficult thing, and the love between a man and a woman was the most mysterious. One moment you're flying above the clouds, and the next, you're buried in the darkness of earthly realities. Love hurts, and if Jesse was just a "player" this could sting. The thought of it scared me, and that's why I resisted.

"Did you know that Santa Monica Beach is one of the most recognizable beaches in the world? It has more screen time in movies than most actors get in a lifetime. They even filmed some scenes in the old TV show 'Baywatch' with Pamela Anderson here."

"Is that so? I can see you're taking your tour guide duties seriously. You know, if this whole fashion thing doesn't work out for you, there's always the travel industry. I hear those Hollywood tour busses make excellent money." He grinned and ducked out of the way in time for my punch to miss his shoulder. "Hey, baby, no need to get all violent on me."

Jesse laughed and wrapped his strong arms around me, pulling me close to his chest. I was extremely conscious of his hard muscles shifting smoothly under his shirt. My nose picked up the light scent of fresh cologne, leaving me powerless to resist; the implications sent waves of excitement thrumming through my body. Each time I was near him, the pull was stronger. He released me and slipped his hand over mine as we walked.

"How's your hand? Is it getting any better?" Jesse had been working out at the gym on an improvised rehabilitation plan that Chase devised to help build muscles and flexibility.

"Actually, it's getting much better. I have more strength in my grip now. Chase is a badass trainer. I didn't think it was possible, but he pushes me harder than anyone. The guy's a fucking slave driver, and it hurts. He says it's for my own good, but I think he enjoys inflicting pain on me." He tossed his head to clear the hair from his eyes and chuckled.

"That's amazing, Jesse. Maybe you'll be able to ride again soon." I pulled our locked fingers to my mouth and kissed the back of his hand. "And your uncle…I really like him, by the way. He's a nice guy and hilarious sometimes. It must be fun living with him." The expression on Jesse's face darkened and he studied the sand as we walked.

"Hey, did I say something wrong?"

"No, it's just…Kenny hasn't been feeling well lately."

"Oh?"

He kicked the sand. "I hate seeing him down and not well."

"You mean like the flu?"

"Don't have a clue. He doesn't either. He's tired all the time and complains that he feels nauseous."

"That sounds like the flu. How long has it been going on?"

"Too long. He's missed a lot of work. I've had to cover for him at the bar, work a lot of extra shifts."

"Has he gone to the doctor?"

"Not yet. He keeps hoping it will go away. You know us men. We don't want to be a pussy and admit we need someone else's help. My idea of treating an illness is to drink myself freaking blind with whiskey and tequila. It's a surefire remedy. Alcohol kills all diseases."

"Ha—it figures you would say something like that. Most guys are like babies when they get sick. I hope your uncle gets better soon, and tell him I said he needs to go see the doctor if this doesn't blow over soon."

Jesse stopped walking and stepped in front of me, putting both hands on my shoulders. His touch was like velvet, smooth and soft. He gazed into my eyes, the light ocean breeze blowing those stray strands of hair into his blue eyes.

"I'm having a great time. I love being here with you. You are magnificent, Niki. I love your heart and compassion, so sweet and caring, thinking of other people's needs before your own." His finger traced down my cheek and caught under my chin. "Every day when I wake up I wonder, how will you surprise me today?" My knees weakened and I felt his hot breath on my lips as he spoke the next words. "Maybe you are just a beautiful fantasy. Kiss me, before you evaporate and disappear." He tilted my chin. Hot tingles shot through my body, as his tongue probed my mouth. He ran his hands up and tangled them in my hair, as we twisted into fiery kisses.

God, it was like he had a remote control that sent me into a lusty frenzy at the touch of a button. It wasn't one thing that he did that spiked me into a dizzy spiral of hot emotions. It was everything, and anything. A word, a smile, a look, and of course "the hair move," the thing he did to push it out of his eyes. That was like drawing the Community Chest card in Monopoly—"Advance to Go" and collect $200. But this was more than just a game. Jesse burrowed into my heart, and this time I was playing for keeps.

If it's true that actions speak louder than words, then Jesse's actions were screaming full blast. My phone blew up with his texts to me. He sent me flirtatious messages, fun messages, serious messages, and I ate it all up.

On Wednesday, Jesse stopped by the pedestrian mall. I met him for a study break in between my afternoon fashion design classes. He stood in the same place where he had smashed his cell phone against the wall, only this time held a pistachio and vanilla double-decker ice cream cone, a little love offering for me. Green rivulets of ice cream melted and dripped down the sides of the brown waffle cone and ran onto his fingers. He said I needed a sugar rush to give me energy for my next class. I licked the droplets of ice cream from his fingers, before taking the cone. How long had he waited in the hot sun? Instead of showing up with flowers in hand, he had dripping ice cream. I loved his original approach to winning over women.

By the end of the week I was in deep with Jesse. How did it happen? I didn't know. If Jesse had his way, he would have seen me every day of the week, but that made me anxious. Only fools rush in. Slow and steady wins the race.

There was no logic to how it happened. We met, I felt that mysterious pull, and that was that. Then I got more tangible information, confirmation that I was headed down the right path. I trusted a little more and now he tugged at my heartstrings.

Saturday night was coming up, and after almost overheating my phone with a gazillion texts and numerous calls, we made plans to go out. This was a really exciting place in my relationship with Jesse, and the thought of sex no longer lingered in the back of my mind. It crashed into my frontal lobe. By the end of the week, my emotions had put out a contract on my logic and any concerns about "dating rules" lost the battle. I threw caution to the wind and said to hell with rules and what other people thought. These were matters of the heart and my heart screamed for Jesse.

I lay in bed each night and traced every inch of his body in my mind, longing for his arms to hold me. I imagined his hands pressing over my feminine curves, willed his fingers to slip inside me, begging him to take me and thirsting for him to devour me with endless hot kisses, laved with his velvet tongue. Fighting this tidal wave of desire was exhausting, so I decided that Saturday night, Jesse would bang the shit out of me.

## Chapter 18 – Frozen Daiquiris

### *Niki*

"What's the name of this place again, Jesse?" I asked. We walked up the sidewalk in Hollywood, to locate the bar where we were to meet Chase and Kat.

"Five O Four. It's right here." A couple of bouncers dressed in black, like Mafia hitmen, hovered near the entrance. Luckily, we found a parking space on a side street several blocks down. With buildings so close together in Hollywood, parking usually meant paying money to use a lot, but we'd rather walk a little than pay.

Five O Four didn't have a real storefront made of glass windows. It was open to the outdoors. The bar itself was small and located in a space shared with a Mexican restaurant, directly across a wide sidewalk. High-top tables were lined up directly opposite the length of the bar, elevated from the sidewalk below, with just about enough room for a waitress with a tray to squeeze between the two. The row of tables abutted a decorative black wrought-iron railing. It was cozy, with a French Quarter, New Orleans, ambiance in its design and decor.

It was easy to spot Kat and Chase in such a small place. They were sitting at one of the tables up against the black wrought-iron rail.

"Hey, you two. Pull up a chair," Chase said as we approached. He stretched a muscular arm up to high-five Jesse over our heads.

"What's on tap tonight?" Jesse asked.

"Their specialty is frozen blended drinks from those machines." He pointed to five large machines built into the wall behind the bar, ensconced in stainless steel. Each filled with a different color of frozen alcoholic drink blends. A metal stirring device slowly rotated behind a circle of glass on each machine. The machines held gallons of premixed alcoholic slushy drinks, ready to pour from a spigot. It was like being at the fair, an alcoholic fair.

"You gotta try this frozen daiquiri," Kat said. Her straw stood erect in thick, light green, blended ice. She pushed it in my direction for a sip. I drew on the straw and a cold refreshing lime flavor shocked my mouth with sour.

"Oh my God. I'm sure to get an ice cream headache from this, but order me one anyway, Jesse. Are you going to try one? "

"Hell, no. Last time I checked I had a dick. That's a girl drink. Real men drink beer, or Jack Daniels," he said with a crooked smile. He grabbed his crotch and jiggled his hand, as witness to his words.

Kat and I shared a look and simultaneously rolled our eyes. I played it off as humorous, but under the table I squeezed my legs together in response to a sharp, delightful tingle. Tonight was going to be "the night," and there he was tempting my patience, looking all fine, drawing attention to the very part of his body I had dreamed about. I struggled to remain cool and composed on the outside, when sizzling thoughts of Jesse's delicious body, and what I wanted to do with it, burned me up on the inside. I squirmed nervously in my seat and glanced to the back of the bar.

*Oh, God. Nerves. Calm down.*

How long did I have to sit here acting all social? I wiped a bead of sweat from my brow and took a long drink of my icy cocktail. Maybe there was a back room where I could rip his clothes off and let him take me right there.

"Niki?" Jesse's smooth low voice was in my ear. "You okay? You look a little pink in your cheeks." Kat slid off her stool and went to the bar for another frozen, slushy drink. I fanned myself with my hand.

"It's just a little warm in here," I squeaked.

"Oh my God, I love this place." Kat "woo-hooed" in her alcohol-infused excitement. She pranced up to our table with a different-flavored drink in hand, the cup

173

dancing in the air above her head. Kat was compelled to sample all of the flavors. "Niki, you gotta try this blueberry one, girl."

I grabbed the high-flying drink above her with both of my hands and lowered it to the table. "Careful, Kat," I laughed. "I *will* taste it, but not all down the front of my shirt."

Jesse leaned in, sporting a huge grin, and pulled me into his side, with a one-arm hug. "Let that shit spill. I'll lick it off your chest." He growled in my ear and planted a teasing kiss on my lips.

No sooner had we sucked down our first round of drinks when a rush of people filled the bar. The crowd was thick and crazier by the minute and every time I moved, I caught an elbow in my side.

Kat squealed and kneeled on the seat of the tall bar chair, waving to the waitress. "Look. They have shots." Kat signaled over the crowd to a young waitress with a filled tray of tiny plastic cups. A clear liquid sloshed in the cups, as she fought her way to our table through a tangle of arms and elbows.

"What are those?" Kat asked, leaning on her elbows, butt in the air. Only Kat could pull off kneeling on the seat of the chair like a child.

"Kamikaze tequila shots. Would you like one?"

"Chase!" Kat yelled to no one in particular. "Get your ass over here. We're doing Kamikaze shots." Kat straightened up on her knees on the stool seat and craned her neck, searching for Chase. The waitress waited for our order, poised with a tray balanced on one hand, in a fashion that begged for a drunken accident to happen.

"Jesse, where's Chase?" she asked. Jesse shrugged, annoyed to be distracted from nuzzling my hair. "Fuck him. He's shit outta luck," Kat barked with mock anger in her voice. "Give us four shots, please. And put it on Chase's tab," she instructed the waitress. Kat spelled Chase's full name, as printed on his credit card, for the waitress. She slid one shot to the side of the table to save for him.

Chase had left the table to talk to a friend and gotten swallowed up by the thick crowd. Eyeing Chase's drink, Jesse threw his back his shot, and said, "I have seen that guy at the gym. He's a friend of Chase's. This beer is going right through me. I'll be right back." He got up and bounced toward the restrooms.

Kat slammed her empty shot cup on the table and slumped back down onto her chair, tired of kneeling. The noise level in the bar was crazy loud. The sound level of the crowd competed with the decibels of the music. Kat and I waited for the guys to return, bouncing to the beat of the music, when a commotion erupted to my right, on the cement walkway, over the black wrought-iron railing. The sequence of events that happened next unfurled with such speed, it was like being in a freaky fucked-up "Apocalypse Now" kind of time warp.

For no apparent reason, a large, drunken freight train

of a guy smashed his beer mug into another guy's face out in the cement walkway between us and the Mexican restaurant. The "other guy" was Chase; he was hit. He threw his hands out, like "what the fuck was that for," startled and obviously blindsided by the move. Chase reeled backwards and the big guy was on him like a Sumo wrestler, hitting him repeatedly.

I barely had time to gasp, when a heavy hand pushed down hard on my shoulder. Jesse had seen the brute beating down Chase and jumped in, like lightning. Jesse propelled himself over our table with unbelievable speed, clearing the table *and* the railing, all in one agile and strategic move, using my shoulder as his launching pad. Never in my life had I seen a body fly over a high-top table like that.

I covered my mouth with my hands, my eyes bulged out of my head. My mind screamed, *"No! No!"* Jesse was like wildfire. He couldn't be contained. He threw the solid force of his entire body at the brute in a football-style tackle. The guy went down hard with a thud, cracking his head on the cement. Jesse didn't stop. He whaled on the guy, pummeling him with angry fists, punch after punch. His exquisitely pumped-up biceps worked like pistons.

"Oh my God! Ka-a-at!" I shrieked in panic.

I bailed out of my chair and screamed at the top of my lungs for Kat to follow. I shoved and clawed at the dense mass of torsos gathered for an audience.

*Oh my God! Oh my God! He wasn't stopping! Make*

*him stop. Someone make him stop. He's gonna kill the guy.*

The rest was a chaotic frozen alcoholic drink blur. Chase lay on the ground, twisting and writhing in pain. "My nose. He fucking broke my goddamn nose!" The spaces between his fingers dripped bright red blood as he curled into a fetal position on his side.

The bouncers struggled to part the tight pack of onlookers. They couldn't tear through fast enough to stop Jesse from doing serious damage. Already down on the ground Jesse straddled him. Jesse's face contorted with grotesque malevolence and I saw that lightning had fists, exploding with rage. Years of pent-up emotions erupted, found their outlet and poured out, like water through a sieve.

"Stop it, Jesse!" I yelled, "Jesse, stop!" But my voice was muffled by the shouts of the crowd and the bar music. I screamed at the top of my lungs, but to no avail. The people in the bar all looked strange and cold to me. They laughed and cheered the gruesome assault like a gladiator fight at the Coliseum.

I stood at the edge of the crowd, numb. My hands covered my mouth with trembling fingers. Jesse's face was like stone, hideous and different. His once deep blue eyes were now glazed over, an icy steel gray. This is what I had feared. The dangerous side of Jesse had come out and was presently in plain view. I was appalled. My hero, my wonderful handsome Jesse, the apple of my eye, had changed and I was terrified.

I was conflicted, seized with the urge to run to him, and at the same moment I was repulsed by him. Reluctantly, I watched and clutched at Kat's elbow, not wanting to look and yet not able to tear my eyes away either. Two bouncers came down on Jesse like a blast from a cannon. One of them rushed Jesse from behind and put him in a choke hold, arching back with convulsive jerks, hoping to snap him out of his fury.

*Oh God, please don't let them break his neck.*

The other one slipped his hands under the armpits of the limp man on the ground and dragged him out of Jesse's reach.

When watching something that violent, it hits you, and you can't help but lose your balance and fall. My stomach turned. I buried my face in Kat's arm, I couldn't bear to watch another second; my heart was hurting for him. The bouncers strong-armed Jesse to the front, and threw him out of the bar. Kat ran to Chase to help him, but before she could get there another pair of hostile bouncer dudes flanked Chase and escorted him out also.

I was unnerved by all this male testosterone-laden bravado. It was hard for me to comprehend why guys bragged after a fistfight. Like it's something to be admired, and if blood was drawn, all the better. As if the blood was a red badge of courage. They enjoyed repeating all the details, blow by blow, like they are professional boxers in the ring. But as for me, I had too active an imagination to handle violence.

In the exaggerated scenario of my anxiety-ridden mind, adrenaline-spiked fear colored and embellished what my eyes perceived. I imagined things worse than they really were. And sometimes, I felt other people's pain in my solar plexus. It was no surprise to me when a sinking emotion soured in the pit of my stomach, as I watched Chase disappear through the bodies.

What an awful night this had turned out to be. I wanted to go home. All my hopes for Jesse and me were dashed the moment the large guy's head hit the ground. It may as well have been my heart that Jesse thrashed into the cement sidewalk. The thought of being in a relationship with a reckless bad boy, who could unleash intense anger at a moment's notice, sent a chill up my spine. This was the proverbial "red flag" that any logical-minded person recognized as a warning. Are some just hardwired to be violent? Or can people change? I bit my lip and looked at my hands, my fingers twisted into nervous knots.

"Come on, Kat. Let's go find them," I said with a heavy voice. Kat frantically pounded keystrokes on her cell phone to get a message through to Chase. She looked up briefly, "Sure, hon. I'm trying to reach Chase. Poor guy, I want to make sure he's okay. Those fucking assholes wouldn't even let me go talk to him." I took her by the elbow. We made our way out of the crowded bar and pushed through a sea of drunken smiles and glazed eyes. She continued to text with her head down and allowed me to guide her, like she was a

179

blind person and I was her Seeing Eye dog.

"The show is over," a bouncer yelled, like the unraveling of my heart was some kind of Vegas show for all to see. The bargoers resumed their festive atmosphere, as if nothing unusual had happened, whooping it up and high-fiving each other with gusto. For them, the fight had been entertainment on the level of an explosive UFC match, but as for me, my opinion of Jesse changed. The door of trust that had begun to open toward Jesse slammed shut with a metallic clang.

Standing outside Five O Four, we searched for Chase and Jesse, but the sidewalk was packed with people. Chase and Jesse were nowhere to be found.

"Oh, thank God," Kat said still looking at her phone. "Chase just texted back. He is okay. They split when they saw cops. Let's go find them."

"You go ahead, Kat. I'm going home. I think I've had enough action for one night."

"What! No, let's—" She paused as she looked straight at me. "Are you okay? You look nauseous."

"Violence makes me sick to my stomach."

"Okay, hon. I'm coming with you. I'm not letting you go home alone."

In the car on the ride home, my phone was buzzing like crazy with text messages from Jesse. Kat glanced over at me with her hands on the wheel.

"Aren't you going to reply?"

I stared at the phone lying in the palm of my hand. I shrugged and pursed my lips. Kat drove on in silence and threw a sidelong glance to check on me, every so often.

"Not talking?" She waited. "You're not mad, are you? Niki, seriously, girl? Don't be mad at him about this. Answer him." She tipped her head in the direction of my cell phone. "He saved Chase, for Christ's sake."

Suddenly, I was overcome with tiredness, exhausted. I didn't have the energy to speak a word, even if my mind could form one. The words stayed like rocks, weighing down my tongue, too heavy to lift, monumental boulders that I couldn't get out of my mouth. I sat that way, head down, staring at the stupid phone. Finally, I switched it to vibrate and shoved it back in my purse. I rolled my head to the side and let it rest against the cool glass of the window, as I stared out into the darkness.

"Niki, don't be like this. He was just sticking up for Chase, defending him. Hell, he had to. That asshole would have put Chase in the hospital. You can't blame Jesse. Chase's friend told me that drunken idiot started the fight for no reason. Chase didn't even know the guy." She peered over at me and then trained her eyes on the road.

I gritted my teeth and closed my eyes. Damn him. Why did Jesse do this to me? He wormed his way into my heart and now this. The pain set in, methodically, it crept over the bright parts of my heart, like a black sinister shadow. It consumed every bit of happiness I had found with Jesse, like a festering, pestilent disease.

I was gripped with fear; panic twisted its hand around my throat and squeezed all the air out of my lungs. The car couldn't get me home fast enough. Although Kat had the air conditioning on high, the air suffocated me. I pounded my finger on the window button, frantic to feel the movement of the wind on my face. I wanted to run, to escape, to fly away.

Kat shoved the gearshift into park at the apartment. She laid her hand gently on my knee and spoke softly, "Niki, girl, things will be better in the morning. You'll see. Everything will look better when the sun comes up. It always does." She wiggled my knee gently.

I managed a meek, pathetic smile and opened the car door into the still of the night. Kat and I threw our arms around each other, girlfriend fashion, as we humped it up the sidewalk to our apartment. Maybe Kat was right. I exhaled a deep breath, once inside the comfort of my own place, and headed off to bed, where I planned to bury my face under a pillow. I needed to process the night's events.

# CHAPTER 19 - Blow

## *Jesse*

"Dude, come on, let's get some blow." I had been working a deal with a skinny-looking chick in an alley. Chase and I had been thrown out of the bar for fighting and I was on fire, my adrenaline pumping like gangbusters. We had to hurry out of there as cops were approaching the scene. Didn't feel like spending the remainder of the night behind bars. When we got back, Niki and Kat had left and to my frustration Niki was not answering any of my texts. What the fuck was wrong?

Chase yanked my arm hard and spun me around.

"No. Are you fucking crazy? Let's go." He wiped dried blood from his nose with the back of his hand. The chick in the alley paced and smoked a cigarette, nervously flicking ashes, as she watched us talking.

"Hold on, hold on, she's gonna leave if I don't go talk to her," I said and wrenched myself free from his grip. I was out of my mind thinking about Niki. The look on her face as the bouncers carried me out frustrated me. I didn't know what the fuck to do, except what I always did in these situations, self-medicate.

Booze worked to a certain extent, but blow was the shit.

I was halfway back to the chick when the powerful thrust of Chase's two hands grabbed me by both arms. He shoved me down the sidewalk in the opposite direction of the alley. It was like a fucking tornado came out of nowhere, lifted me off my feet and flung me against the brick walls, spiraling me down the storefronts. After I stopped bouncing off the walls, Chase walked me farther away from the alley, squeezing my arm in a fucking vise grip and hissed in my ear. "She's an undercover cop, you idiot."

He dragged me along like a disobedient puppy, as I looked back over my shoulder. I could tell from his face that it was no joke. "How the hell was I supposed to know?" He threw me a glance like I was a fucking moron and let go of my arm with a push that made me rock back on my heels.

We stopped in front of a dingy sports bar and stood on the sidewalk eye to eye, breathing hard.

"Tequila shots, on me."

"No more drugs, promise? You'll never get Niki that way, man."

"I'm an asshole. I promise." I jerked my head in the direction of the door to a dive bar, and Chase shoved it open with one hand as we went in.

*~*~*

*Why the fuck doesn't this house stop spinning?* I

staggered into my bedroom, groaned, and fell face-first onto the bed after another night of meeting with my therapist, Jack Daniels, this time joined by his fellow colleague, Jose Cuervo. Old habits were rising up like blisters these days, and drinking myself blind was a damn good strategy to kill the pain. In hindsight, it was a piss-poor idea, but I didn't give two fucks about shit. It had been three days since the fight and Niki still hadn't answered my texts or taken any of my calls. I even went to her place but no one answered. What the fuck was her problem? Was she mad at me over the bar fight? Shit, it wasn't even my fault, and...Fuck! I just wanted the world to go the fuck away.

The bed was shaking. Was I still drunk? Or was this a damn earthquake? What the hell? The shaking didn't stop.

"Get up, Jesse." A loud voice invaded my drool-laden sleep. It got louder. "Jesse." And more demanding. "Get the fuck up!"

I was facedown on top of the covers in the same position I had left myself the night before.

I rolled over and squinted to see the outline of my uncle. He strode to the window and tore back the blinds, making them rattle in the most annoying way. I groaned and covered my eyes with my forearm. "What the fuck did you do that for? Shut that shit."

"Get up outta that bed. It's nearly noon. I've had enough of your bullshit behavior. Get your ass up, and take a fucking shower, you smell like puke." He spat the words as he threw a bath towel at me. *Damn.* His voice had a sharpness I had never heard before. "When you're done, come to the family room. We need to have a talk." He stormed out of my room. *Jesus.* I had never seen my uncle act like this. What the fuck was his problem?

I dragged myself into the bathroom and showered. My head was splitting, like it had been hit with a wrecking-crane ball. The search for aspirin drove me out to the kitchen, where Kenny stood waiting for me with a pot of strong black coffee.

"You look like shit." He pushed a cup of coffee across the counter in my direction.

"Thanks. You look like hell yourself," I snapped back.

He pursed his lips and took a sip of coffee. "I'm gonna ignore that remark."

"Sorry, I'm a dickhead." I winced as another hangover hammer-blow exploded inside my head. "Do you have some aspirin?" I asked with squinted eyes.

"I should just let you suffer, you little son of a bitch, teach you a lesson. But yeah, I'll get you some." He turned and opened a cupboard near the sink. "Listen, Jess, we need to talk."

Aw, shit. He wants to talk. What's to talk about? I'm an asshole, end of story. But I complied and planted my ass on the big overstuffed chair, next to the brown leather couch, in the family room.

"Here…" He extended his hand, palm up, with three

pills. I swallowed them down with a mouthful of coffee.

"Jesse, I'm not one for beating around the bush, so let's cut to the chase. You have been fucking up, man. You have been drunk for three days straight and ditching work. I don't like it and it has to stop."

My uncle was a man of few words when it came to getting something off his chest. He placed his cup on the coffee table in front of us, in a definitive gesture. He leaned back and folded his arms across his chest. I sat and listened, hoping like hell the pounding in my head would ease up.

"I know you like that girl Niki, and I know she is not talking to you because of what happened at the bar with Chase. Yes, you were helping a friend, but you can't solve all your problems with booze and violence. Women don't go for that shit."

"Women fuck with my mind. I don't understand them at all. Maybe it's too late for change." I leaned forward with my elbows on my knees, holding the coffee mug between both hands.

"You've got too much negative energy in you right now. You need to grow that shit the fuck out of you. Getting drunk doesn't solve anything; it just defeats your goals. If you want Niki back, you are going to have to change; you will need to show her that you *have* changed," Kenny said.

I hung my head and listened. I didn't know what to say—he was right, this was all about Niki. All I wanted was Niki back in my life, and not pissed at me for being a dickhead.

"Why do you keep doing this, acting like a fool? You never used to be this way. I used to be so proud of you. Hell, you had a great career, winning races and shit. I taught you how to ride and you made me so proud. Everything was going good in your life. Now you just let it all go to shit. What's going on inside your head?"

I flung myself back against the couch and stared at the ceiling, fighting the urge to zone out and withdraw. Putting my feelings out in the open, on the line, was damn uncomfortable for me. "Thing haven't been going well..." I mumbled. God, that sounded like a weak-ass excuse.

"I thought you were over all this...this drinking and recklessness once you came here, but now...I don't know, Jesse. I don't know." He shook his head sadly. I felt like a jackass. I had let him down. "You've got to get your shit together. You have to be responsible for your own actions."

"I, I..." I blew out a long breath and got up the nerve to spit it out. It was painful, all this soul-searching shit. It may be all well and good for pussies, but it's not my style. Glancing at him, I knew I had to explain. I drew in a breath and paused for a second. "I just want Niki back. That's all. That's what makes me act all crazy-like and go ballistic."

He pursed his lips and nodded solemnly. His

features softened as a glint of recognition appeared in his eyes. "I see. So, you think she might be the one? She's that special?"

"She's a fucking angel." I threw my hands out to the sides. "I get all high and shit whenever she's around and I can't stop grinning like a stupid Cheshire cat."

"Hmm. You feel light and happy when she's around?"

I nodded. He had a twinkle in his eye as he talked and a hint of a smile tugged at the corner of his mouth.

"Like you can't think of anything else when she walks in the room? Like you can't breathe without her?"

"Yeah, yeah. That's *exactly* it. How did you know?" My uncle was the goddamn Albert Einstein of love.

"Yup, sounds like you've got it pretty bad for her." He chuckled.

"But she won't even talk to me. What do I do now?"

"First of all, going on drinking binges doesn't work. Cut down on your drinking, control your anger, and show Niki that you've changed. I'm not saying you have to stop drinking completely, but Christ almighty, boy, you don't have to make it a way of life. Give her a little time to cool off and I think she'll come around once she sees the old Jesse, the real Jesse, the Jesse that I know."

I jumped to my feet, my head still pounding from my hangover. "Kenny, I think you are right. I'm gonna go win her trust back. I don't have a damn clue as to

189

how, but I'm gonna do it."

I stepped a little lighter as I retreated to my strategic planning room, AKA my bedroom. The dark gray storm cloud that had been raining on my parade finally lifted. I was stoked.

# CHAPTER 20 – What Happens In Vegas...

## Niki

"You're moping. Stop picking at your sandwich." Kat scolded and shoved the large half of a turkey and avocado on sourdough into her petite mouth. Kat joined me today at my favorite sandwich shop on my break between my fashion design classes. Right outside this very shop, Jesse had brought me the ice cream cone study break treat. Out there he first showed up, unannounced, to "stalk" me, then smashed his cell phone as an excuse for being at the mall.

Most of my sandwich sat untouched on my plate. I teased half a red tomato slice out from between the slices of bread, lifted it to my lips, then let it drop onto the plate.

"I don't even want this." I sighed and wiped my fingers on the napkin. I rested my chin in my hand. Why the hell was I so drawn to Jesse?

"Have you heard from him today?"

"Is the Pope Catholic? Of course, he's begging to see me. He texts me day and night...well, he backed off for a while, but he got his second wind." I pushed the plate away. Kat set her sandwich down, her fingers still wrapped around it, a sure sign that a lecture was about to ensue. She stared me in the eyes with one of her serious "big sister" looks and leaned forward.

"I totally don't understand you, Niki. Give the guy another chance. He was defending Chase. We've been over this before and...I've seen how he looks at you. God, it's like your shit don't stink, girl." She laughed.

I broke a smile at Kat's attempt to sway me, but...if I went back to Jesse wouldn't I be following the path to my own destruction? "Oh, Kat. Guess who sent me a message last night?" Her eyes went blank. She'd never guess, so I blurted it out. "Hot guy from Vegas."

Kat's eyes widened. "Shut up. You mean Trevor? What does he want?"

"He wants me to go out with him."

"I thought he lived in San Francisco." She sucked on the straw in her drink.

"He's in town on business or something."

"You're not seriously thinking of going out with him, are you?"

I sat up straight and jutted my chin out defiantly. "I am."

She slumped back down in her chair and took another sip, "You're sick. I can't believe you would even waste your time," she said in an even voice.

"I can do what I want; besides, I need to get my mind off Jesse," I said indignantly. "Trevor will be like a test. He will be my litmus paper. I'll go on a date with Trevor and see how it compares to when I'm with Jesse." I felt damn proud of myself for coming up with this idea.

Kat crumpled up her paper napkin and threw it on her empty plate. "I think it's stupid but whatever. Do what you feel you need to do." She stood up, leaned over the table and took one last sip, then gave me a hug. "You know I love you. I gotta go. I have a rehearsal in about… minutes ago." Holding her large Coach purse in the crook of her arm, she flung her trash into the garbage and pushed the door open with her backside.

I fished my cell phone out of my purse and opened the text message from Trevor that had been waiting. I responded that I would love to get together. What harm could it do? I justified that it would get my mind off Jesse and help me think clearly. Jesse blinded me. He was exciting. He was dangerous. And I had decided to steer clear of him for a while for my own good.

*~*~*

Thursday night rolled around and I was ready to put my plan into action. I wanted to meet Trevor at the restaurant but he had insisted on picking me up in his rental Mercedes. I didn't even know you could rent a

Mercedes, but I didn't like the idea of him picking me up. I wanted to keep it casual and if the date went bad, I wanted to be driving my own car.

As the waitress seated us, I moved clumsily, first stepping in front of him, then cutting in from the side, bumping into him. I told him, "Excuse me," and failed to land in my chair gracefully. It was a stiff beginning. I was out of my element. But despite the initial awkwardness, I was determined to make the best of it. Or so I told myself, as I sat across from him, wringing my hands under the table.

"Good to see you again, Niki." He jangled the ice in his scotch on the rocks and drained it. "What have you been up to down here in SoCal, the land of the crazies?"

"Um, wow, nothing much, just mingling with the other *crazies* here. What's wrong with Southern California? Does everyone from up north act like this part of the state is a foreign country?"

"It may as well be," he pointed out self-righteously. "You talk weird, like, you know, like, like, like. And everyone is so vain. The women are fake with all their hair extensions, and everyone wants to look younger than they are. Jesus Christ, they dress like sluts, and the guys think they're surfer dudes." The waitress placed another scotch on the table. I sipped my wine. Things were developing splendidly.

I chewed on the celery stick from my salad, bearing down hard, to grind out the bitter taste forming in my mouth.

"Excuse me. I need to use the ladies' room."

"Sure, sweetheart. Hurry back." He downed his third scotch and slammed it on the table. He pushed his chair back and half stood up, as I turned to find the restrooms. I left the table and felt his stare burn a hole in my backside, assured that he was getting an eyeful of my ass. I pushed into the ladies' room and leaned up against the wall. As usual, Kat was right. This was stupid. What the hell was I thinking, agreeing to go out with this guy? The thought of climbing out the bathroom window occurred to me, except this restroom didn't have one. I decided to suck it up and try to politely make it through dinner, then bail.

I came out of the restroom and gave a tug on the hem of my short skirt. I hoisted my purse over my shoulder and looked up to a searing pair of blue eyes. My heart jumped.

"Jesse. What are you doing here?" I hissed. He leaned on the bar with a Jack Daniels, neat. I scowled and leaned close so Trevor wouldn't hear or see me, though he was halfway across the main dining area.

"Hey, Niki. Nice to see you too."

"Are you stalking me? Again? How dare you? That's so wrong. I'm on a date. How did you know I was here?" I asked through clenched teeth.

"Who's to judge what's wrong or right? Maybe I *am* stalking you. I have been known to be guilty of it before." He leaned casually on the bar. A playful smirk turned up the corner of his mouth.

"Kat told you I was here, didn't she? I'm gonna punch her in the arm next time I see her, the little snitch." I glared at Jesse and realized the desire for him ricocheted through my veins. I should be mad at him, I *wanted* to be mad at him, but deep down inside I was thrilled that he was here.

"Look, Niki. What are you doing here with that doofus over there?" He set his drink on the bar and slid off the stool to stand next to me, so close that I felt the heat emanating from his body. He pierced me with his gaze. The intensity and truthfulness of his stare rendered me helpless.

"Just tell me why you are here, Jesse?" My voice trembled.

"I came because I need you. I came to beg for your forgiveness. I had a talk with my uncle and I realized something. I know I scared you and I'm so sorry. I shouldn't have gone all apeshit on that guy." He leaned in even closer and his emotions filtered through his eyes. "Please, Niki. I'm gonna turn over a new leaf. I'll do anything for you."

The sincerity in his voice melted me even more. I looked down silently at the granite bar top, white knuckles gripping the strap of my purse. I held on like it was the sole tether to my sanity, fearful that if I gave in, I might slip into an unpredictable world with Jesse. I threw a nervous glance back over my shoulder. Trevor was waiting at the table. I wasn't sure if he could see me.

"Actually, I'm glad you showed up. Things weren't going so well with Trevor over there." I pointed with my eyes.

"I'm here for you, baby." He slid his hand over my forearm; his touch ran smooth and warm across my skin. I sighed. With his head bent down close to mine, his intoxicating musky scent swayed me. I closed my eyes and whispered, "Can you take me home?"

"Of course. Let's get you out of here. Go tell him you changed your mind, and let's leave. Or do you want me to tell him?" He stroked my arm, the breath of his words fluttered in my ear.

"No, I'll tell him. Just give me a minute." I pulled away and returned to Trevor's table. He was texting on his phone and hardly noticed me.

"There you are. I thought you had gotten stuck in the toilet." He chuckled.

I managed a faint smile. "Sorry, Trevor, I gotta take off. I'm not feeling well. Thank you for the dinner...and I'm really sorry."

"Wow." He looked me up and down. "Can you at least wait until I'm done eating? Then I will take you home."

"Don't worry. Stay and finish. I can get myself home. Bye." I turned and walked towards the exit.

# CHAPTER 21 – Defeated

## *Jesse*

Niki and I stood on the curb, as we waited for the valet to bring my truck around. The guy Niki had ditched on her date approached from behind. "What the fuck is going on here? Niki, who is this?" he asked in a gruff voice.

I dropped Niki's hand and turned to address him. "Take it easy, man. My friend is not feeling well, so I am taking her home. Just go back to your dinner," I said.

The valet pulled my truck up to the curb. Halfway between us and the restaurant, the dude stopped in his tracks and yelled. "Bitch, really? You're leaving with another guy?"

Niki's eyes widened and her mouth fell open. Before she had a chance to respond, he launched another insult.

"You're nothing but a cunt and a cock-tease!"

His words froze me in my tracks. "What did you say, motherfucker?"

"I said your little girlfriend is a fucking cunt."

I turned to Niki and spoke as calmly as possible, but under my skin my blood boiled in my veins. "Excuse me, can you wait right here for a second?"

"Ignore him, Jesse. Just take me home." She reached for my arm.

I bolted back, fronting him. His face was red from his shouting. "I thought that's what you said." My breath came quickly now. "But you know what? I totally forgot something." I was now close enough to see sweat beads forming on his forehead.

"What did you forget?"

"I forgot this." I wound up my fist and without warning launched it square on his jaw. As he hit the ground I shouted in his face, "That's no way to speak to a lady. Learn some fucking manners, asshole."

I left the dude groaning into the pavement and turned on my heels to take Niki home. Niki was gone. I raced to the corner, my eyes scanned the sidewalks, but she had vanished like a fucking magician. I grabbed my head with both hands. "Fu-u-ck!"

*~*~*

## Niki

"What the hell happened last night?" Kat popped out of the bathroom and padded down the hall to the kitchen in her pink pajama pants. I poured a cup of coffee in her favorite mug and pushed it across the white tile counter in her direction.

"Jesse's an asshole. I don't know why I keep thinking he is worth pursuing. He hasn't changed at all." I slid the half-and-half in her direction and stuck the handle of a spoon out for her to take. "He showed up at my date with Trevor, thanks to *you.*" I wasn't really mad at Kat for tipping him off. My real anger was at myself. I was weak and allowed Jesse's charm to pull me in. "It happened all over again, like déjà vu of that Five O Four place when he got in a fight…well, this time he didn't go completely bananas, he just punched the guy. I think."

"Oh my God, Niki. You have men fighting over you. That's so cool."

I rolled my eyes. Kat had a unique way of looking at violence.

"Kat, it's the same behavior. He's solving his problems with violence and I don't know if I can handle a guy like that." I looked down at my coffee and stirred it again with the spoon. "What if I'm his problem one day? Is he gonna freak out on me?"

"No. Are you crazy? That guy adores you. Why did

he go off on Trevor?" She took a seat on the stool and leaned her elbows onto the counter, intent on hearing all the details.

"Everything started a little weird with Trevor…well, he was being a jerk, actually. Halfway through the date I went to use the restroom. When I came out Jesse was at the bar waiting, or stalking me, thanks to you. Well, I talked to him and…" I exhaled a breath. "God, Kat, I really do like him. I don't know what he does to me, but he's got my heart. That why it's so hard. How can you have such strong feelings for someone, yet despise part of his behavior?"

"Honey, no guy is perfect. So what did you do?"

"I caved. I melted right there under the stare of his dark blue eyes. I said, let's just get the hell out of here and we left. We got outside and that's when Trevor came barreling out the door yelling a bunch of shit, like I was a cunt and how dare I walk out on a date with him, blah, blah, blah."

"Wha-a-at? He called you a cunt?" Kat slapped the countertop with her palm.

"So when Jesse heard him call me a cunt, he walked right up to him and punched him. I was so freaked out I ran away and took a cab home."

"Jesus, Niki, are you fucking crazy or what? Jesse loves you like no one else. Of course he would punch him for saying that. And quite frankly, if I was in your shoes and someone called me a cunt, I would demand my guy to stand up for me. Jesse's your knight in fucking shining armor, girl." She cocked her head to the side.

"You don't think that shows he's a whack job? Unstable?"

"Hell no! He was defending your honor. What did you want him to do? Just let the guy get away saying that shit to you? No, I'm telling you, Jesse is not a psycho, nutcase kind of dude. He may be impulsive—and damn hot—but deep down, he's really a good guy. He's passionate about the things he believes in and has a hard time expressing it in words. But most men are like that."

"Do you really think so?"

"I *know* so. You need to stop all this wishy-washy, namby-pamby 'I don't know if I can handle him' bullshit and claim him before another girl gets a chance. He wants you more than anything else in the world. He worships the goddamn ground you walk on, sweetie. Even Chase says so."

"What did Chase say?"

"Why don't you ask him yourself?" Kat pushed my cell phone across the countertop until it was under my nose.

I pursed my lips and turned my chin up to the side. I raised the cell phone and called Chase. My heartbeat picked up its rate, as I waited for him to answer.

"Hey, Chase. It's Niki."

*"Hey, Niki. What's up?"*

"Are you at work?"

*"I'm always at work these days. What do you need?"*

"Um, I need your advice on a matter, but first, is Jesse there? Cause I don't want him to hear—"

*"No, Jesse's not here. As a matter of fact, he's home right now packing. He is going back to New York."*

My heart dropped to the floor. I turned and looked at Kat and she mouthed the words, "Oh my God." She had heard everything.

"He can't leave…" I blurted out. Desperation rose in my body. The air was sucked out of my lungs. My mind screamed the word, NOOOO! But my mouth said, "I mean, moving back to New York? Why? I thought he was here all summer, helping at the bar?"

*"Niki, I'm gonna level with you. The guy is in a hurt locker. He told me he messed things up with you again so he's throwing in the towel. He's leaving, Niki. He might even be gone already, for all I know. If you care about him, get your butt over there before it's too late and talk him into staying."*

"Can't you talk to him and convince him to stay?"

*"No, only you can do that. He's broken right now. I've never seen him like this, Niki."*

My hands trembled as I placed the phone back down on the counter. Tears stung my eyes. I swallowed hard and cleared my throat.

"Kat, what should I do? He's leaving."

"Do you really like him?" she asked in all seriousness.

"Yes," I squeaked through tears spilling down my face.

"Then go. Go, girl. Tell him how you feel." She tugged on my arm and pushed me towards the door, grabbing my purse and keys along the way. "You will be losing a great guy if you don't hurry."

I stumbled along, sniffing and wiping tears with the back of my hand as I went. I paused before I shut the door. "Thank you, Kat. I love you, girlfriend."

She snatched a tissue from the box on the counter and waved it in my direction. "Here, wipe the mascara from your eyes."

As I peeled off towards Kenny's house, I took a deep breath and gripped the steering wheel tighter, hoping it would steady my trembling hands. My mind raced. What should I say? What if he refused to talk to me, slammed the door in my face and told me to get the fuck out? Maybe I could go with him to New York? Oh, shit. What was I thinking? I can't leave my classes and my life here for him? Oh, yes, I can. I can do whatever I want. I never realized what I had with him. He was right in front of me the whole time, and like an idiot I almost missed it. I figured it out; now it was clear.

I steered my car to the curb and cut the engine in front of his uncle's house. I fussed over texting him first to let him know I was on my way, but was afraid he would say "don't come." I swallowed hard and made my way up the driveway to the door. I passed by his black, big-wheel pickup truck. A pang of nervous desperation pierced my heart as I saw two boxes loaded in the bed of the truck.

*Oh shit, oh shit, oh shit. I can do this.*

I shook my hands out, like a boxer about to enter the ring. My nerves rattled me to the bone. I jabbed the doorbell with a trembling finger and waited. *One-Mississippi, two-Mississippi, three-Mississippi...* I was counting the seconds. It was a nervous habit I had to distract my mind from overwhelming fear. When the door swung open, I audibly exhaled.

"Niki." His voice sounded surprised and his face revealed it as well.

I closed my eyes and swallowed hard. "Um...I...was just, driving by..." I turned and waved a hand, palm up to my car. "And thought I'd stop and say hello." I bounced up and down on my heels, pursed my lips, and nodded my head. I had rushed out without a thought for what I was wearing. I glanced at my plain white tank top. Not exactly dressed to sway someone's heart, but it would have to do.

Jesse shot me a sidelong glance, eyeing me up and down. "Whatever you say. Come in," he said, and swept a hand in a welcoming gesture. At least he didn't slam the door in my face. I was nervously wringing my hands. I grabbed onto my purse strap and practically tiptoed past him, brushing close enough to his powerful chest to remind me why I was there.

Once inside the family room, I stood awkwardly in

the silence of the house. His uncle must be at work. There was no sound except the ticking of a decorative round clock on the wall, and the pounding of my heart was drowning it out.

"Can I get you something to drink? A Coke or bottled water?" He strode over to the kitchen, paused in front of the refrigerator, and rested a hand on the door handle.

"Oh, no thanks."

Jesse pushed his unruly hair out of his eyes. The move was my Achilles heel, the move that drove me crazy watching his muscle ripple and flex under the tattoo. Was he that calculating? Or an Adonis who didn't know his own power? I dipped my chin to my chest and cleared my throat, hoping if I didn't look up, it would release me from his magnetic pull. I had to get this out. I had to say it.

"Jesse, I'm just going to say it straight out. I came because I heard you were leaving, moving back to New York." I shifted my weight from one foot to the other. He walked forward and stood, leaning, one hand on the breakfast bar and the other on his hip.

"Yeah, I plan on leaving in the morning."

"Oh, I see." I took a couple steps towards him, licked my lips, and swallowed hard. "Well, um…what about us?" I cocked my head slightly to the side.

Jesse closed the distance between us in two strides and held both of my hands. Dipping his head, he looked in my eyes. "Niki, I'm sorry, but after I saw you last time, I figured I'd fucked up one too many times and you would kick me to the curb. I thought that 'us' was over. I can't stay here, if there's no chance for us. This place...this city will always remind me of you. So, the only thing for me to do is go back to New York and get my life back together."

His eyes pierced mine and we connected. The floodgates opened and I struggled to pull it together.

"Jesse, I don't want you to go. I don't give a damn about the fights. I need you here. Don't go."

"Why should I stay? You don't even see how much I've changed for you. I fought for you; I stood up for you, Niki."

"The violence scares me. I don't want a man to control me. I want a man to work with me. You know I've been dominated my whole life. But I do believe that you care for me and you mean everything to me. You came into my life and filled a huge hole in my heart. Ever since my mother died, I have had a hard time feeling anything, until I met you. I don't know how it happened, but I feel connected to you and if you leave, I don't know how I can go on and...and..."

I talked fast and rambled in an attempt to say everything I wanted. The more I spoke, the more his features softened. He cupped my face in his hands and looked deep into my eyes. It rendered me breathless. His eyes flicked up and down from my lips to my eyes and back again.

Before I could catch my breath, he claimed my

mouth with his; tears welled up behind my closed eyelids. He pulled back enough to let me feel his breath on my lips. "I'll stay, Niki," he whispered. "I'll stay for us."

Tears spilling, and my chest rising and falling from my irregular breathing, I choked out the words, "Thank you, Jesse. That's all I want. Just give us a chance."

He crushed my mouth again, swirling his tongue, pushing his hands first up into my hair and then running them down my back, pressing me up against his warm muscular body. Granting fate to follow its path, I leaned into his embrace and met his kisses with unabandoned submission, my mind whirling, all thoughts lost to the moment. In that one simple movement, that one willing gesture, all of his wishes and future wishes were affirmed. He knew I was his and he was mine. He pulled back from our kiss, and dipped his head to touch my forehead, still holding me in the crook of his elbow, his arms wrapped around me so tight, while I trembled.

"I will, Niki. You are my sweet angel, so beautiful and good. I never had much faith in love, until I met you, and everything changed. I don't want to imagine a life without you, so now the old me has disappeared. You are everything I've been looking for. Every kiss and every touch feels new, yet so familiar. When I look at you I see an angel." Tears rolled freely down my face as I blinked up into his eyes.

Jesse loosened his vise grip and put enough space between us for him to bring his hands to my face. He wiped away my tears with his thumbs; his burning gaze never left mine.

"I need you with me." Goose bumps raised on my skin, as he caressed me. Before I could catch my breath, he ran his hands down my arms and took my hands. He pulled on them, as he walked backwards, driving me towards his bedroom, our eyes never unlocked. With the weight of his body, he pressed my back against the hallway wall, as the solid pack of his chest muscles firmly compacted my breasts. It ignited a torrent of heat that ricocheted up and down the entire length of my body. I felt the hardness of his erection against my thin tank top and sweat shorts. My nipples budded up in immediate response. He interlaced his fingers in mine, palm to palm, and pushed my hands over my head. I was pinned to the wall. My arms went up, my chest arched out, and my head tilted back, reflexively. He held my petite hands tightly. I released a soft whimper and my lips obediently parted for him. He claimed my mouth hungrily, as if he were a man starved of every basic human need, darting his velvet tongue in and out of my mouth, and sucking my lower lip as he pulled away slowly. Heat pulsed in my stomach. He pushed with his knee and coaxed my legs apart. A long hot tingle raged between my legs.

Jesse trailed hot kisses down my neck, his free hand ran up the inside of my thigh, and then all the way to where it pushed the crescent of my breast into his kisses. I rolled my head to the side and looked down, tantalized by the sight of his mouth working my breast. I watched, as the tattoo on his bicep danced to the tune of his tugs, pushes, and squeezes, until the pink of my nipple rewarded his tongue. I groaned a deeply salacious moan and whispered Jesse's name into the late afternoon shadows of the hallway.

The loose soft cotton fabric of my sweat shorts moved compliantly as his hand slid down inside my panties. He crushed his lips to mine as he slid his fingers easily between my separated, wet folds, ratcheting up the delicious tingle that he had already activated in me. He kissed and fondled me, his tongue and fingers moved in synchronicity, in and out, swirling, pushing, and stroking two frenzied erogenous zones at once. My mind screamed, overwhelmed with pulsing sensations that assaulted my ragged nerves. My breath caught, as he pushed his fingers inside me and every last coherent thought spilled out of my brain. He pulled his fingers out of me, and pulled back, his breath ragged with desire. He pinned me with a gaze from his burning blue eyes. He looked at me from beneath those long unruly locks and anointed himself with my wetness, like holy water.

In a hormone-infused fog, we stumbled the rest of the way into his bedroom, pawing and tearing at unwanted clothing. Jesse kicked the door shut with his foot, his hands slipped up under my flimsy tank top and pulled it off over my head in one swift sweep. The shock of having me alone, nearly naked, for his pleasure, registered like a ten on the Richter scale. He paused for a moment, stunned as if in disbelief, drinking in my body, roaming and caressing every curve with his eyes. I slowly slipped my bra straps off, first one shoulder and then the other. I pulled my arms out, one at a time. I held the cups of the bra to my breasts with splayed fingers, pushing and squeezing for his viewing, teasing his adrenaline level to the max. I looked down at my breasts, pushed them up hard to overflow the cups and lifted my eyes to catch his reaction. It was magnificent. His eyes were so hungry, the expression on his face like an open book. He wanted me badly, as much as I wanted him.

As if suddenly released from a frozen time warp, he blinked and ripped off his T-shirt over his head and let it fall to the floor. He exhaled a slow breath. My eyes flickered and widened, his muscles rippled under his tan skin. I raked my teeth over my lower lip. My eyes trailed down to the bulge in his jeans. I closed my eyes and swallowed hard. He pushed his hand through his hair, pulling my attention back to his inked bicep, and slowly unraveled any last ounce of resistance I had left in my body. I wanted him to fuck me. I wanted it so badly, more than anything I'd ever wanted in my life.

I threw off my bra and wiggled out of my shorts, leaving on my hot pink lace panties for further tease appeal. He leaned forward like he was about to reach for me, but I planted my palms flat against his chest, in a signal to wait. The warmth of his skin permeated my palms and my fingers splayed with anticipation across his tight pecs. They jittered, then stilled. I looked into his eyes. I lightly trailed my fingers down his chest, his abdomen, and stopped my tactile exploration at his belt buckle, as I lowered myself to my knees.

Jesse's jeans came off, boxers and all, and his hard cock sprang free, a magnificent piece of artwork of the male body. I circled my hand around it and stroked his flesh, while cupping his balls. He hissed and tossed his head back. I wrapped my warm wet lips around his engorged manhood and sucked. I squeezed his balls, sucking and stroking. He put his hand gently on my shoulders. He grabbed my hair and tousled his hands in it, guided it and moaned with delight. He gently pushed my head back to release his cock and smiled at me. "Ladies come first." He lifted me by my arms and guided me to the bed.

Laying me gently down on its softness, Jesse kissed my stomach right above my panties, then enjoyed the tease, as he pulled them down over the curves of my hips. All of my nakedness was in his total view and I could hear his excited breathing.

For a very long time, his warm hands moved along my thighs, tracing up and down, and each time he strayed towards my wetness, I moaned louder and louder. I couldn't help it. I had wanted him to touch me like this since that first night on the beach. He sucked my nipples, using his other hand to guide each one, budded with pinkness, into his mouth, and gave equal attention to both.

Jesse's mouth slid down my ribcage, down my stomach and to my mound. I gasped, flushed with anticipation. Using his fingers he parted my folds and flicked his tongue on my pulsing clit. I bucked against his mouth, wanting more.

He licked and fingered me, building the intensity. I tensed and he fucked me with his fingers, as my orgasm took reign over my body, building, climbing, and accelerating, nearly to the exploding point. I looked down and the second I saw his head moving between my legs, pleasuring me so erotically, I wailed and my orgasm came with a sharp edge to it, crashing and shattering me to pieces.

Jesse rose up to his knees, stroking his cock, priming it for action. I saw in him an intensity so great, a desire so wild, that I thought I couldn't take any more. He leaned over to the bed stand and ripped open a small foil packet. A moment later, he slid into me, filling me, and delicious tingles of pleasure rocketed through my entire body. He groaned, and panted with the satisfaction of finding his destiny. His rhythm picked up, with each thrust and I moaned louder and louder, my body bucking and writhing in response. I pulled my legs up, bending my knees to offer him the deepest penetration. I longed to please him completely. I felt the pull again. I couldn't believe it. He was making me come a second time. I was transported, I was out of my mind, out of my body with sexual pleasure.

Repeatedly screaming out his name and God's, in gasping breaths, I dug my fingers into his flesh, frantically I positioned him where I needed for the second orgasm. The wave of tension rose, then broke, and I was taken with such ferocity that it resembled convulsions. He growled and released deep inside of me, shaking and trembling, as his hot breath fell in steamy puffs on my neck. Collapsing onto me, he exhaled a final long audible breath and rolled to the side, waiting for our breathing to regulate.

Jesse leaned over, stroked my hair, and looked into my eyes. "Baby, that was amazing. *You* are amazing, everything I've ever wanted."

I tried to swallow the heavy knot in my throat. Uncontrollable tears threatened my eyes.

"Hey, now. What's this?" he asked. His voice turned soft, as he leaned up on his elbow and touched the tears now springing from my eyes. "No crying allowed when you're in Jesse's arms." He kissed my cheek and brushed away the wetness with his thumb.

I gave a short laugh. I felt ridiculous for being so emotional. "Don't worry, they are tears of joy. That was so intense just now. You shook me to my core. I don't usually trust someone, well, guys that is, so easily. But with you, Jesse, I feel safe, like I can trust you with my heart. You've opened up something in me that has been closed for a long time and it hit me really hard right now. That's why the tears." I smiled and looked up into his eyes with a long-deserved happiness. I was convinced I saw the same returned in his look.

The slant of the afternoon sun had moved the shadows on the wall. I had totally blown off my classes for the day. Schoolwork had completely left my mind, but now a glint of guilt stung at me. Despite the fact that we both could have easily lingered in the throes of lovemaking all day, we decided to get up.

I put my clothes on while Jesse stepped into the adjoining bathroom. I sat on the edge of the bed, dressing, and gazed around at the moving boxes he had started packing, grateful I had gotten to him in time. My eyes stopped on what appeared to be old books and memorabilia that his uncle had stored in this room before it became Jesse's bedroom. The fact that his uncle had not completely removed his belongings was a sharp reminder that Jesse's stay in California was only intended to be for a couple months.

There on the wooden bookshelf, wedged between a small family Bible and another book, was a worn green photo album. The thought of discovering old photographs of Jesse as a child piqued my interest and I reached for the album.

I sat down on the edge of the bed and gingerly opened the album, careful of its dried plastic page covers, now brittle and yellowed on the edges with age. I smiled as I turned page after page of old photographs. I recognized some with a much younger and quite handsome version of Uncle Kenny. Pictures of smiling faces, arms around shoulders, family vacations, and kids on dirt bikes. It looked like New York State.

Jesse walked out of the bathroom, saw the album, and rolled his eyes with a groan. I was dying to have him confirm my notion that the photo I had my finger on was him and his mother, with such a sweet and innocent face looking out at the camera. I couldn't wait to rib him about being "mama's little man." Guys hated this kind of stuff. Girls loved it.

"Who's this?" I pointed to a photo of a little boy standing in front of a calm lake, wearing jeans and a T-shirt. He held a fishing pole, with something hanging on the end of the line, and had a big smile. Jesse stood in front of me and examined the page.

"Ha. That's me as a kid."

"Aww. You were so cute."

"Look how small that fish is." I leaned in for a closer look.

"What fish? I don't see a fish."

"Right there." He pointed to a tiny fish dangling on the end of the line, about the size of a minnow. His finger moved to another photo. "Look, here's a picture of my 65cc bike. That was such a cool bike. Jimmy and I made our own dirt racetrack on our property. Man, we had a blast."

"Is this your mom?" I traced my finger across a woman's plastic-covered face. The photo, a professionally taken headshot of a smiling woman with long flowing hair, was marred and dingy, as if at one time it had been rescued from the bottom of a trash can.

It had a crack that had once been a fold, whose sharp-creased edges had curled up over years. It curved up and separated the surface of the photo into a tiny crevice that ran diagonally across the lower portion of the photo, straight through his mother's heart.

"Yeah." His voice softened and he stared at the page, like he recognized something familiar in the curve of her smile.

"She's very pretty. I can see you have her smile."

Then he opened his mouth and the hurt that came out astounded me.

"She…never got over my dad's death. She has been sick for a long time."

"I know, Jesse. These things are so difficult. How did your father die?"

"A car accident. I was only eight at the time. That's when my uncle came to live with us for a while. "

The weight of his story sat heavily on my shoulders. "I'm sorry. I didn't mean to bring up sad memories."

"It's okay. You know I carry a lot of guilt about my mom. I should have been there to take care of her, not halfway around the fucking world racing. Maybe she wouldn't have done it. It all happened so fast. One day she was fine and then next, she overdosed on her depression medicine."

"It's not your fault, Jesse. People don't do this kind of thing out of nowhere. There's always an underlying reason. A person can't watch over someone twenty-four-seven. Don't blame yourself."

"You don't understand, after my dad died and my uncle left, she became much worse, she became clinically depressed. Jimmy sort of took over and became the man of the family, helped me and my mom. My brother and I swore that we would never abandon her like the other men in her life."

"That's a lot of responsibility to put on a child. How old were you when your uncle left? Ten? Did she see a therapist when her depression first started?"

"Yeah, that's when she got some pills and it seemed like she got a lot better, at least for several years. It wasn't until after I left and started touring and racing all over the world that she fell apart. If I had stayed put she wouldn't have tried to end her life."

"I know you said you never went to a therapist...well except for 'Jack Daniels, ' but you need to fire him and see a real therapist."

"I would never do that."

"I could go with you. I can take you to my therapist. You really need to talk to someone who can help you work through your feelings, otherwise the guilt is going to eat you up."

"I didn't know you had a therapist. Why would you need one? You're perfect, Niki."

"Ha, you're cute, Jesse. Listen, do it for me. I'm sure your mom is proud of what you have accomplished with your racing."

"Maybe, I don't know."

"This is something a counselor can help you

understand. Please, say you will try it."

"Okay then, I'll give it a shot, but I don't think it's going to work."

I looked at the picture of his mother again and hoped I would meet her someday. I probed at the album page, pressing with my finger. It felt thick.

"What's this?"

He leaned over for a closer look. "I'm not sure."

"It feels like there's something behind the picture, it feels thick, like a paper."

"Let me see." Jesse took the album from my hands and pulled a folded, yellow paper from behind the picture of his mother. "It's a letter."

Jesse unfolded the dry stiff paper to read. I could see cursive letters written across the width of the page and all the way down, to fill the front side, but the angle at which I was sitting didn't allow me to read the words.

"A letter?" I could barely contain myself and curiosity jumped in my veins.

Jesse's face dropped as his eyes scanned over the black ink.

"It's a love letter." His voice was low and flat.

"How sweet. From your dad to your mom?" He looked up from the page and his eyes met mine.

"No. From my mom to my Uncle Kenny."

My eyes widened, but I didn't want my expression to be taken as judgment.

"Apparently my uncle and my mom were in love with each other at one time."

219

Jesse dropped his hand with the letter to his lap. He stared blankly into a corner of the room and allowed this new revelation to sink in. He blew out a short breath and pushed his hand through his hair, shaking his head. "Wow. That's fucked-up. I can't believe my mom and my uncle...I mean, did they...was my uncle banging my mom? Right in our house? His dead brother's wife? What a prick. I thought he came to help, not take advantage of her...asshole. I thought he was a good guy and now...What the fuck?"

Jesse's agitation caused his voice to rise in pitch and the words came faster. I reached over and put an arm around his shoulder.

"I'm sorry, Jesse. But don't jump to conclusions. It could have been a secret love and though they had feelings for each other, they didn't act on it."

Jesse stood up and paced back and forth, unable to contain his anger; it spewed out all over the room as he raged on. "What an asshole, what a pervert. We were kids, Jimmy and I, just kids. We looked up to him, we trusted him...I , I loved him. He took care of us, he taught Jimmy and me things we needed, things boys needed. Fuck, I have to talk to him, confront him. That's what I have to do. I have to know the goddamn truth, even if it kills me."

Jesse waved the letter in the air as he spoke. Hurt and confusion burned in his eyes. "Jesse, everyone wants to hold their parents to a higher standard, like they are gods, devoid of human vices. We've all done that as a coping mechanism, we idealize our parents, in our mind, to make life more acceptable. Keep an open mind. Give him a chance to explain. "

Jesse folded the letter and shoved it in his jeans pocket. I closed the album and placed it back on the bookshelf. The tension in the room pushed me towards the door.

"You need to talk to your uncle, so I'll get out of your hair, but let's talk more about this later. You should take some time to process the information. It's a lot to handle. Come over to my place after work and we'll have a long talk. It will help to vent and get this out of your head." I stood in front of him and searched his face with my eyes. I felt his hurt, right in my solar plexus. He placed his hands on my shoulders and took a deep breath.

"Okay, Niki. I'm sorry for getting so upset about this. You're the greatest." His voice slowed to a normal pitch. "I'll come over later. Thanks baby."

Jesse took my face in his hands and kissed me, soft and sweet, a sign that things were good with us and we could move forward in our relationship, despite the latest bombshell. He walked me to my car. As I stood there to say farewell, he pushed a strand of hair out of my face. He kissed me again and sent me on my way.

I pulled away from the curb with my heart torn in two directions. I was elated, happy, floating on air about my relationship with Jesse. He agreed to stay in California and I had just had the hottest, most outrageously best sex I'd ever had in my life. However, I was all too familiar with Jesse's coping mechanisms. He promised me he'd changed, but old habits die hard. And I worried about how he would handle this new turn of events with Kenny.

# CHAPTER 22 – The Test

*Jesse*

"Where the hell is he?" I threw open the door and stormed into the bar, the betrayal letter burning a hole in my pocket.

Chase looked up while he wiped the black bar counter with a white rag, in large sweeping strokes from side to side.

"Who's that?"

"My uncle. Fucking Kenny."

"Whoa, dude. You sound pissed."

"Just tell me where the hell he is."

"I haven't seen him for hours. He came in, said he had a doctor's appointment and hasn't been back. Have you tried calling him?"

"Shit, he's not answering. It goes straight to his voicemail." I rubbed the back of my neck with my hand. Tension pulled at every muscle in my body. Where the fuck was he?

"I hope you're here to work. There's a shitload that

needs to be done. The set-ups need to be refilled, glasses need washing. I could use the help, man." He gave me a strained look and wiped his hands on the rag. "I know he's your uncle and all, and I don't mean to be disrespectful, but it's getting ridiculous how much time he's missing from work. I try to cover it, but seriously, something's gotta give. I'm stretched to my limit here." He threw the rag under the counter and walked to the other end of the bar. My uncle had done a good job of turning me against him and now he pissed off his employee. I had to find him, this shit couldn't wait.

"Sorry, dude. I have to find out what's going on. You're right, this shit sucks. I'm going to get to the bottom of it. I'll help when I get back, I promise, Chase." He didn't turn around and continued to wash glasses behind the bar. I yelled over my shoulder, from the doorway, "I won't let you down, Chase, just hang in there for a couple more hours and I'll be back."

I flew out the door, and pounded my way to the truck. I peeled out of the parking lot and my big wheels jumped the curb. I floored it and headed to the house. I was on a mission to find Kenny and get to the bottom of this. Something was fucking rotten in Denmark and I had to know what it was—right now.

Kenny had never mentioned the name of a doctor but I figured I could go back to the house and search for a clue. He had a habit of opening his mail and throwing it in a pile on a desk with the house phone. I might find a bill, or some paperwork bearing the name of a doctor or

224

clinic. Why was he missing so much work? And the love letter. I still had the fucking letter to deal with.

I slammed my truck into park in the driveway and flew into the house oblivious to everything around me. My mind sifted through thoughts, possibilities of where I could find a clue. I checked my cell phone again. Nothing.

I came down the hallway, my eyes still glued to the phone screen, and there he was, sitting on the couch, bent forward with his head in his hands. What the fuck? Was he crying? Did someone die? I froze in place at the edge of the family room, holding the stupid phone like it held all the answers.

"Uncle Kenny. Are you okay? Feeling sick again?" I asked.

Kenny straightened and looked at me with tired watery eyes. "No, no. I'm fine. Just thinking. Going over work schedules in my mind. Come in and sit down." He motioned for me to sit.

"I talked to Chase and he said you went to a doctor's appointment this morning but didn't come back. What's going on, man?"

"Nothing. I got a little tired and must have fallen asleep here on the couch. I woke up when you came in. I'm just a little groggy from sleeping, that's all. I was about to go back to the bar. What's going on? Did you want to see me?"

"As a matter of fact, I do have something I need to talk to you about."

I pulled the letter from my jeans pocket and threw it on the glass-topped coffee table. Ugly thoughts reared up in my mind and feelings of betrayal threatened to sting me like a cobra, but I had to know the truth. Kenny was my hero

"I found this in that old green photo album on the shelf in my room. It was stuck behind a picture of my mom."

The crumpled yellow letter laid on the smoky, glass-topped table, as out of place as the awkwardness in the room. "Oh shit, I thought I got rid of all of those." Kenny rubbed the back of his neck and winced. "I suppose you've read it," he said.

"Goddammit, is it true? Did the two of you…hook up? You would have to be a fucking snake to do something that low." I spat the words. Angry and hurt feelings burned like acid in my stomach, and with every fiber of my being I hoped that somehow It wasn't true.

"Jesse, calm down. Listen…" Kenny began, and exhaled a long breath. "Years ago, before you were born, back in high school, we were friends, me, your dad, and your mom, all three of us. That's how it started; we were all best friends. We went to the movies and high school football games. We went on trips together to the lake. Everything was great, it was fun, right up until that fucked-up day."

"What fucked-up day?"

"When your mom told me she was pregnant. I knew the baby couldn't be mine because…well, we were just friends. She told me it was your dad's. Your grandma was furious. She said they had to get married, so they did, and shortly after, Jimmy was born. You can imagine what that did to us, hell, we were just teenagers. And then, life became serious, too serious for your dad. He ruined everything, couldn't handle it, the baby, and the responsibility. He started drinking too much, flirted with other girls, and your mom became secluded and withdrawn. It continued until your dad died.

"Your mom broke down completely. She was in no shape to handle two boys all by herself, so she asked me if I would help and be there for you and Jimmy...so I did. That's why I came. I came for you and Jimmy and your mom, of course. I owed it to her; I mean, she was still my best friend."

"So when did she write this letter?"

"Sometime after I left you guys. We were getting too close and I couldn't do that to the memory of my dead brother. I tried explaining it to your mother, but she wouldn't listen. She sent many letters, but Jesse, trust me, nothing ever happened."

"But there is one thing I don't get. If nothing ever happened and if you didn't have any feelings for her, why did you keep this letter?"

"I forgot it was there, thought I'd gotten rid of them." Kenny threw his hands in the air.

I wasn't sure how to handle Kenny's explanation. Part of me was relieved, but it had changed how I thought of my mother. It was odd to think of her as a teenager with an unexpected pregnancy. To me she was a saint, devoid of any human vulnerability, but now I realized she was only human. A crapload of shit had been dropped on me since this morning. Hell, I was packing to go back to New York and now…fuck. I leaned forward and put my head in my hands.

The trill of Kenny's phone broke the silence. He placed the phone to his ear like it was made of brittle glass. The puff of air from his movement blew the crumpled paper and it fell to the floor.

"Hello. Yes, this is he. I see. Yes. Yes. I understand. Will my health insurance cover that? Okay. Thank you."

He ended the call and I slowly lifted my head from my hands. Kenny's face was white. He looked tired and spent. He let out a long breath and carefully set the phone on the table. He looked drained in an instant, and something pulled at my heart. How could I be mad at him when he looked so pathetic?

"Who was that on the phone? And don't say nobody. You look like you just got kicked in the balls by a horse. Now tell me. What's going on?"

Kenny stared in silence for a moment and leaned back, tilting his head against the couch. He spoke slowly and deliberately, letting the words float out into the ethers of the room, like black ghosts that filled the room with darkness.

"That was my doctor. I have cancer."

What the fuck—I shrunk in my seat. Words wouldn't come to my mouth. The only word that formed in my mind was "fuck."

*Fuck, fuck, FUCK! FUCK!!!*

First Dad, then my mom and now my uncle? How much more fucking pain was life gonna deal me? My goddamn mouth was dry and my throat closed up. It felt like a large hand wrapped around my neck, choking the shit out of me. I squeezed my eyes shut, to avert the urge to throw anything and everything within my reach. I wanted to bust up something really bad. I forced myself to keep myself under control. It wouldn't do any good to act a fool in front of Kenny. A thousand questions burned in my mind, but I couldn't bring myself to ask, so I just said the next most stupid thing.

"What kind of cancer?"

"Leukemia. It's a cancer of the blood." He signed a long breath. "I wasn't going to tell you, or anyone, yet. But I can't do this alone. It kills me to have to be weak, to need someone else's help but…"

"I don't know what leukemia is, or what it looks like when someone has it, but what can I do to help? Do you want me to take over at the bar while you get better? I mean, what kind of treatment will you need?"

"I need a transplant."

"Like a lung, or kidney, or what? I could do that, give you one of mine. If it's a kidney you need, well, mine might be kind of pickled from all the booze but…"

229

"It's not like that, Jesse. I need a bone marrow transplant. I need someone who is a perfect match, or else my body will reject it. My own immune system will think it's invading my body, as a threat to my system, and my body will kill it."

"Oh Jesus, Kenny." I ran my hand through my hair, brainstorming a strategy. "That's no big deal. We can find a match. Maybe I'm a match. Someone will match."

"I'm sorry, Jesse, that's very noble of you, but the doctor said most of the time a perfect match comes from a person's children, and I never had kids."

"What about a close relative?"

"Like a brother? I only had one brother, your father, and he's dead, remember?"

"What about a nephew, like me or Jimmy? How do we find out if we are a match? What do we have to do, cause I'll do anything."

"Maybe, but doubtful. I already asked the doctor. Nephews are not a good possibility, only a slight chance of being a match. Don't get your hopes up, Jesse."

I was afraid to ask the next question. "And if you don't find a match…"

"Well, if I don't find a match, then it's all over, my life is done."

"What about taking medicine, like pills of some kind, or radiation, or chemotherapy?" I had heard about these treatments on the TV news, but the report I saw made it sound awful. I was desperate to help, but I was running out of ideas.

"None of that will save my life, there's nothing, only a bone marrow transplant."

"How do we find out if I'm a match? What do I do?"

"You go give a sample of your DNA."

"Oh shit, how the hell are they going to get that? That sounds kind of scary."

"No, it's not." He laughed a weak laugh. "I believe they take a swab of the inside of your mouth with one of those giant-sized cotton swabs. I think you'll survive."

It was a relief to hear Kenny laugh. Despite my initial shock, I was ready to fight for my uncle. I wasn't a fucking quitter.

"I'll do it. Tell me when and where. I'm your man, and if it helps, I'll get Niki to do it, and Chase, and Kat, and all the friends I can think of. There just might be a match among one of them, you never know."

"I can't thank you enough but it's still going to be a long road ahead of me and I hate to ask you for even more than you've already done. I'm going to need your help at the bar and if I don't get a perfect donor match, well..." He took a deep breath.

"Don't even go there. Don't even think that way. Set up the test with the doctor or whoever and let me know the time and place. I'll be here."

"Thank you, Jesse. You are a good kid, I mean a good man."

"Just promise me one thing, Kenny, don't keep secrets from me ever again. We are family, families don't keep secrets."

Kenny and I sat in silence for a few minutes. Then Kenny slapped his hands on his thighs and attempted to get up off the couch. "No sense sitting here feeling sorry for myself. There's still a shitload of work to get done today at the bar." The fatigue of his illness kept him from standing and he fell onto the couch. Goddamn, I hated seeing him like this.

"Easy, Kenny." I sprang to my feet to steady him. "Why don't you stay here and get some rest? I can take care of everything at the bar tonight."

"Nah, nah…" He attempted to wave me away, intent on rising again, but the exhaustion on his face told the true story.

"Damn it, Uncle Kenny, you're not going into work tonight. Let me and Chase handle it." He surrendered and succumbed to the soft cushions of the couch.

*Where the hell was Chase?*

This bar wasn't going to run itself. The set-ups still needed to be prepared and I was up to my neck in liquor re-orders. I raised a bottle of top-shelf vodka to the light and eyed the contents through the glass. This was the last bottle and it was nearly empty. I slammed the bottle back in the rack. My nerves were scratchy, like steel wool.

*Shit. Where the fucking hell was Chase?*

The silence in the bar was interrupted by impatient rattles and clinks. I was in a rush to prepare the bar for the day's business. I heard the whoosh of the back door. Chase was late.

I called out over my shoulder and continued to wipe the bar top with a white rag, "About time, asshole."

A female voice answered, "That's no way to say hello to your girl."

I dropped the rag and strode over to meet Niki, as she popped out of the back hallway. "Hey, baby. I thought you were Chase."

"Do I look like Chase?" She grinned.

"He was supposed to be here half an hour ago, that asshole. What are you doing here at this hour?" I kissed her lightly on the lips. "Shouldn't you be in school?"

Niki dropped her books and tote bag on one of the tables, and snaked her arms around my neck.

"Don't call Chase an asshole. He's my friend." She stuck out her lower lip in a pout. It made me want to suck it into my mouth.

I circled my arms around her waist and said, "I meant it with love. He's my friend too, baby, but it's just that I'm up to my neck in shit here." I tipped my head and touched my forehead to hers. "I'm glad you stopped by to see me. But I'm afraid I really can't take a break right now."

"No need to take a break, I came to help out. I'm

ditching school the rest of today."

"You are a lifesaver, baby. What would I do without you?"

I pulled her in and tasted her lips for a long kiss, breathing in her delicate floral scent. My nerves relaxed, as she leaned into the kiss. She felt so damn good in my arms with her petite body pressed against mine. She pulled away and let her hands rest on my shoulders, giving a little squeeze and massage.

"Wow, you feel tense, Jesse." She continued to knead my shoulders. I pulled away and moved to the bar to organize the glassware. Niki slid onto a bar stool opposite me to talk while I worked.

"I'm tense because I have a ton of shit to do and this place stays open long hours. It's not a 'nine to five' kind of job. Then with Kenny being sick and all…" I threw down the knife I had picked up for cutting lemon wedges and pulled my cell phone out of my pocket.

"And I have no idea where Chase is." I checked my messages—nothing. I slid my phone down the slick surface of the bar, as frustration pricked at my nerves.

Niki's eyes followed its path, growing wider as it went. She could tell I was pissed.

"Wow, you *are* on edge. How is the situation with your uncle, by the way? Have you heard anything from the test; I mean, do you know if you're a match to be a bone marrow donor?"

"It's been four fucking days now. You would think they would work overtime to get the results as fast as

possible. For Christ's sake, a guy's life is at stake here."
I ran my hand through my hair and picked up the knife
to cut lemons. "If I'm not a match, Jimmy said he
would be tested too."

"That's good. I can't wait to meet Jimmy."

"Oh, he's very different than me. He was the good
kid, I was the black sheep." I shook my head and
managed a laugh. Niki sat with her elbows propped on
the bar, sucking on a red candied maraschino cherry she
plucked out of the garnish tray.

My phone moved, as it vibrated to an incoming call.
I looked in the direction of where it had come to a stop
and dropped the knife.

"That better be Chase." I wiped my hand on my
jeans and stepped down to answer it.

"Hello?"

*"Hi, this is Nurse Rosen from Scripts Hospital. Is
this Jesse Morrison?"*

"Yes, I'm Jesse Morrison." My heartbeat picked up.

*"The results of your bone marrow test have come in
and we have good news."* She sounded cheery and I
realized I had been holding my breath.

*"You are a perfect match for your father."*

"Ah, that's great. But you mean my *uncle,"* I
corrected her.

*"No…"* She paused for a few seconds, as I heard her
shuffling the files. *"The results of the DNA test clearly
state, Kenny Morrison is your biological father."*

My stomach wrenched as the world suddenly fell out

from under me. I looked straight into Niki's eyes to anchor me as I responded, "Ms. Rosen...You're fucking kidding me, right?"

*To be continued in Fearless – Jesse Book 2, out NOW!*

If you enjoyed this book, please help spread the word. Tweet about it; message your Facebook friends and tell anyone else who might also enjoy it. Most importantly of all, if you could, I would love a personal review on Amazon or Goodreads by you. It really helps.

I'm so excited to hear what you think about the book, so please reach out to me on Twitter http://twitter.com/evecarterbooks or on Facebook http://facebook.com/evecarterauhor.

Much love,
Eve xoxo

# Acknowledgement

First, I would like to thank all of my readers. Without you, my books would not exist. I truly appreciate each and every one of you. I would also like to give a big "shout out" to the girls in the Smutty Book Whore Mafia on Facebook. You girls rock! Without your connections and support, Deceived wouldn't have had such a good beginning. I enjoy the humor and candor with which we interact, not to mention the awesome photos. They give me lots of inspiration for writing my steamy sex scenes. I especially want to thank Dawn Martens and Andrea Gregory for beta reading Breathless. Your edits and comments have been incredibly helpful.

A big "thanks" goes out to all my Twitter followers and Facebook friends, all several thousands of you, who keep me tweeting into the wee hours of the night.

Finally, I would like to thank my editor and book cover designer, Primrose Book Editing and Design. Thanks for all of your help and clever ideas.

# About The Author

Eve Carter is a true romantic at heart and with a modern contemporary erotic twist to her romance novels, you had better fasten your seatbelt, as the ride is always fun, exciting and fiery.

Living in Southern California, but a mid-westerner at origin, Eve finds plenty of inspiration for her books in her own exciting life. Eve has always loved the arts and as a young girl, she took dance classes and spent the summers reading books from the local library.

Fascinated with the written word and its power to guide the imagination, Eve started writing short stories and later took Creative Writing classes in college. Eve graduated from The University of Iowa with a B.A. in Journalism and an M.A. in Higher Education.

Made in the USA
San Bernardino, CA
04 December 2013